Lily in the Mirror

Lily in the Mirror

PAULA HAYES

First published 2016 by
FREMANTLE PRESS
25 Quarry Street, Fremantle WA 6160
(PO Box 158, North Fremantle WA 6159)
www.fremantlepress.com.au

Consultant editor: Naama Amram
Cover design and illustration: traceygibbs.com
Printed by Everbest Printing Company, China.

National Library of Australia Cataloguing-in-Publication entry
Hayes, Paula, author.
Lily in the mirror / Paula Hayes.
9781925163872 (paperback)
For primary school age.
Family secrets—Juvenile fiction.
A823.4

Fremantle Press is supported by the State Government through the Department of Culture and the Arts.

Government of **Western Australia**
Department of **Culture and the Arts**

Publication of this title was assisted by the Commonwealth Government through the Australia Council, its arts funding and advisory body.

For

Josephine Lois Thompson

and Charlotte Josephine Hayes

— big love.

One

I have started this journal in the hope that something interesting and supernatural will happen to me but I fear this is unlikely. I am not an orphan and I do not live in a cupboard under the staircase. We do have a staircase cupboard — it is full of gumboots and old newspapers but I don't live in it and I have parents, two of them. Alive. And they both love me. A lot. This is good but annoying, as it is usually unloved orphans that have all the magical luck. Mum actually gave me a cushion with 'You are so loved!' written on it. I was like, what is this … I wanted the one with the black leafless tree lithograph on it. It looks dark and mysterious. To be dark and mysterious is one of my lifelong goals. If passing inhabitants of an alternate magical world see the 'You are so loved!' cushion on my bed, they will keep walking.

When my dad comes home from business trips, he tries to read to me books like *Matilda* (best book ever) but I am getting a bit old for it and I point kindly to my hardback series of Harry Potter with the ADULT covers so he will understand I am quite literate and stuff.

I also have two sisters and tragically … one brother. None of us can guess which one is Mum's favourite because she loves all of us so much — even Pig Boy slash the male sibling. Annoying MUCH? It's a love festival at our house. We range in age from twenty-four to eleven, with me being the youngest. I am the fourth child of an only child (named John) and a third adopted child (named Letty) who has no idea about her birth family, which I must say does give me hope in the dark-and-mysterious department. If I were Mum I would really want to know that sort of thing. She could be royal or something. My mum is special but she could be authentically special. I really love Kate, Wills, George and baby Charlotte. They are sooooo lovely and I just know George is going to be an awesome big brother, unlike the Pig Boy that resides in our house.

There are only two of us loved-up kids living at home at the moment, so sadly we look like a really typical family. *Typical* — this is a terrible concept, I hate typical. It is the exact opposite of interesting and unusual.

I live at home, naturally, as I am only eleven years old. My brother Linden (AKA Pig Boy!) is fourteen. He hates me and he lives at home. And then there is my twenty-two-year-old sister Fern. She is an Arts student who kind of lives at home when she is not cat-sitting. I find it disappointing that she has never looked after a black cat — now that could be interesting as it might be a 'familiar', which is a witch's magical lifelong pet. But no, they are all silvery blue or ginger; typically (shudder) they are a very boring stripe. Fern is not in residence at the mo — YAY. She always hogs Mum with her stupid love-life problems.

My eldest sister Zinnia is aged twenty-four. Zinnia has moved to Spain to be with her Spanish fiancé Manuel. They are both working on a big engineering project. This is very exciting except Zinnia is not excited about it because she is so boring. Mum has to send her Vegemite, bulk Cherry Ripes and Smith's Crisps in a large box every month. When she skypes, Zinnia always ends up crying. I feel like saying, 'YOU ARE SO LUCKY TO BE IN A DARK AND MYSTERIOUS PLACE! Go and explore a Gothic basilica and eat some tapas and stop crying for heaven's sake.' But I don't. I am mature that way.

I am being packed off to my grandfather's down south for two weeks because my parents are going away to celebrate their twenty-fifth wedding anniversary. They go away every year at this time and they think it is funny to say they pretend they do not have four children for two weeks of the year. Hilarious. NOT.

Fern has to come home with the three cats she is minding to mind Linden. Mum says it is to keep Linden 'company' as her strapping lad certainly doesn't need taking care of, but then I overheard Dad say that he does not trust Linden to not burn the house down as he is 'easily stimulated' and 'easily led'. Mum replied that Linden is going through a 'difficult stage'. This stage is fourteen years long with no end in sight. Then I heard Mum say that she can't believe people trust Fern with their cats and there is no way she would leave Fern in charge of me AND Linden while he is 'journeying through his special challenges' which is like … being the best BULLY he can be.

It's not that Mum doesn't adore Fern — they are like besties with all their sickening girlie chat. It's more that Fern forgets stuff like food and hygiene and is not very observant of the Pig Boy bully 'going for Olympic gold'. She is not ordinary and is what Mum calls a 'free spirit'. You would think this would make me like her more. It doesn't. She is sooo self-involved. Bleurghhh!

So back to me … I overheard Dad say a break from Linden would do me the world of good and that next term they should seriously think about enrolling me in a fun young people's dance class like funked-up jazz hip-hop so I can meet new people.

NOT HAPPENING IN THIS LIFETIME, FATHER DEAREST!

So it's Grandad and me for a fortnight. He is so ordinary it makes me want to sigh. He makes jam and has a jam collection. JAM! Thirty different combinations with fig, it's not even something sexy like strawberries. It's a yawnfest. But he is a dear sweet thing and I do love him a lot. And I love his house. And he is big on food and hygiene. He makes a cake every day — a lot of times the cake contains fig, which is vomitous, but every few days he pulls out a hazelnut and chocolate cake with GANACHE and it more than makes up for nibbling politely on figgy loaf. Mum and I once tried to make the chocolate cake at home but it was a disaster and this made Mum cry.

Back to the house — Grandad's house is the oldest in the street by a long way. It has pretty stained-glass patterns around the front door and roses that are older than Dad. So they are ANCIENT! Their branches are like … gnarled and as thick as sausages. When I was little I thought they were magical and spent a lot of time crawling in and between them. I was looking for fairies (blush!) but all I got was scratched — rewrite: severely hacked to pieces — and Grandad would chase me around with some homeopathic ointment that probably contained stewed figs.

So food and hygiene covered.

I am taking this journal of course. I am enjoying writing with my new pacer but I am on the lookout for a quill or a fountain pen. I am also taking my laptop because it has all my novels and stuff on it. Grandad doesn't have an internet connection so I won't be able to google new words to learn — which is my all-time favourite hobby in the world! Grandad says his eyes are too weak now for a computer, but when he stays with us in Perth he always manages to enjoy searching for designer cake recipes or the value of coins in his coin collection.

I won't write any more until we get to GG's. This is what we call Grandad, thanks to Zinnia.

Zinnia, Fern and Linden … their names are woody, weird and embarrassing. We are all named after plants. I guess Dad is into gardening and Mum is into babies. They must have imagined Linden would grow into a wise talking tree. Wrong.

And then there is me … I am Lily (so glad I didn't get stuck with Fern), which is the same first name as Harry Potter's mother, and my surname is Griffin, which is pretty close to Gryffindor — so I think this is a good omen that I could be a chosen one in some sort of way. EXCITEMENT!

Two

On this visit to Grandad, I am going to concentrate my paranormal investigations in the Rosy Room across from the kitchen. We call it the Rosy Room because the walls are covered in faded pink rose wallpaper circa nineteen-forty-something. It's creepy, I'm sure I can feel a weird vibe coming off it, which is very Potteresque of me. I'm quite drawn to vibes. I love the word *circa*, it means *around about*! Actually I love all kinds of words. According to the Pig Boy I am a nerd and a word-freak. WHATEVER!

I asked Grandad about the wallpaper and he said it was a bit before his time. He said the house belonged to Grandma's family first and then he and Grandma inherited it. Our name for Grandma is Nimmy (thanks Zinnia ... NOT). I would like to ask her what is up with the creepy room off the kitchen and I also have a lot of other inquiries about stuff. But Nimmy does not have the answers anymore. She lives in a nursing home three streets away. Grandad visits her every day. She has a sort of dementia.

Sometimes she remembers Grandad and on those days he is very happy, and sometimes she even pretends to remember me, which I think is incredibly kind of her since she got ill when I was around six and she couldn't possibly connect that gorgeous child with this beautiful preteen. Still she tries, she tells the nurses, 'This is my granddaughter,' and because she has three granddaughters I feel it is a pretty good guess, which I think means she is still in 'there' somewhere. But my dad thinks she is 'gone'. I do not like it when he says that. I think it is 'incredibly simplistic' (Dad is always saying this) and quite rude but then, she is his mother and he would kind of know that sort of stuff. But seriously, it does upset me and I wish he wouldn't say it.

When I look at all the beautiful pictures of Nimmy in her younger days (she was so beautiful back then), I get a very sad vibe. I also get a very sad feeling that I do not look like her. AT all.

I am now at Grandad's house. I am unpacking and Grandad is cutting up the cake. It is a plain vanilla butter cake and there has been no mention of fig whatsoever. Yay!

The cake was delicious (no surprise) and Grandad has slipped off his Italian loafers and is having a nap. Grandad is a bit 'dapper'. This means he is neat and stylish.

I am going to examine the Rosy Room for interesting and mysterious stuff. The key to the room hangs on a hook right next to the door so it will be easy to get into. Apparently Nimmy wouldn't let anyone in and the key went missing for a long while. GG found it recently and put it back where it belonged. GG said it is a bit of a storage area for things Nimmy couldn't part with. Sometimes I stickybeak around when GG unlocks the door to find one of his coins or stamps. It has a lot of old furniture and boxes and tins and clothes, so something a bit vintage and antique might show up — which is my second favourite thing next to dark and mysterious.

Okay, my hand is shaking. It is literally shaking. I HAVE FOUND SOMETHING. It took me a while to work out exactly what it was I found, because it was hiding under some old letters and cards in an old chocolate tin. When I began to have a suspicion about what it was, I did not want to touch it. I have to confess that at first, I let out a little squeak and dropped the tin of letters onto the floor.

I snuck into the kitchen and Grandad was still snoring in his chair by the old range, warm from cooking the cake. I got a pair of tongs and went back to pry off the letters and cards.

My hand wobbled around a lot and I kept thinking it couldn't be what I thought it was — because that would be crazy and highly unlikely. These two things are always good indicators that you are onto something a bit special and supernatural.

It is what I suspected.

It is a finger.

A FINGER!

Sickening. I had to leave the room and go into the kitchen again. I nearly woke up GG but he looked so old and tired I didn't have the heart. So I sat down and ate another slice of his most excellent cake. I waited at least ten minutes and then I began to feel 'calm from the carbs' (Fern says this as she stuffs her face — now she has the muffin top to prove it) and my brain started to work again.

This is it.

This finger is my calling. This finger is my destiny. So I am going to investigate it and use the surrounding facts to build a picture of how a finger has come to reside in an old chocolate tin in the Rosy Room.

Later in the day …

Okay … so this is really freaky and I am feeling a chill as I write this. The finger is fresh. If that is not creepy enough, the cards and letters from the chocolate tin are dated 1945 to 1952. I have read a couple of them for clues. They don't seem to contain any. They are like:

> *Dear Lucy,*
> *Happy Christmas 1950, so lovely to see you again. Keep strong.*
> *Love, Uncle Don and Aunty Ena.*

I know Lucy is my grandma that we call Nimmy, but who is Beryl?

> *Dearest Beryl,* *April 1946*
> *May I trouble you for your simply delicious jam-filled sponge recipe? I also adore your mock cream …*

Not riveting stuff, although the mock cream recipe does intrigue me.

The papers are yellowing and stuck together and there are a couple of black-and-white photos of two girls and a cat. (Not black but stripy — SIGH! Sighing is so Zinnia.) If the finger was put in the tin all those years ago, wouldn't it be all black and green and blue with dried blood and, more than likely, wouldn't a bone be sticking out?

This finger is pink and all dewy. The nail is quite pretty and clean. There is no dirt under it. The lid of the tin was really hard to get off and I had to get a metal letter opener out of the desk drawer. It took me ages and I stabbed myself twice but I felt compelled to finish off the job, as I was very drawn to the tin. I think I might have a gift and my gift is telling me that the finger has been there a long time. But my eyes are telling me the finger looks … I don't know how to say this … the finger still looks alive.

Grandma Nimmy has been in the nursing home for four years and so it is just Grandad GG here. My powers of deduction tell me Grandad must be responsible for the finger. It is quite probable that he cut off someone's finger. Maybe he has even murdered someone. Maybe he is not my grandad but an evil *doppelganger* (which I'm not sure how to pronounce but it means *a look-alike* on the outside but totally different on the inside). I am really feeling sick now and should not have eaten the second piece of cake.

Grandad has just opened the door and popped his head around the corner and asked what I want for dinner. I actually had the presence of mind to answer, 'Fish fingers,' and I watched his face really carefully. He slapped his hands together and said, 'Yummy! Let's do wedges with that, Lily Pilly!' like he was really looking forward to fish fingers and wedges with his youngest and favourite grandchild. I have to listen to my intuition (because I have a gift) and it tells me Grandad is not a murderer but my awesome GG.

PS GG is the only one who can call me Lily Pilly.

Three

Before we got the fish fingers and stuff at the shops, we walked around to Nimmy's Home. She is no longer beautiful. In fact, and this really pains me, she is quite unattractive. She has crusty freckles that are now the size of planets and her front tooth is missing. There was an incident with a gingersnap biscuit recently. Apparently she is not to have them anymore as she 'can't manage them' and nobody is sure who gave it to her. Dad was really cross about it.

I don't like to look at the gap but find I can't stop. She didn't know Grandad or me today. I could tell Grandad was sad and he went off to find her missing underpants that were clearly labelled. Sophie, our favourite nurse, stayed for a minute and asked me what I was reading now — she so gets me. I said I had just finished the Anne of Green Gables series. She said that series was an ALL-time favourite. Even though it is not supernatural at all, I like it … it is still a really good read. Anne is such a crack-up.

Last holidays I had just finished *Harry Potter and the Deathly Hallows* and we had a discussion and stuff on it. It was great to meet a kindred spirit. Sophie's favourite character is Dumbledore. Her second fave is Ron Weasley. Sophie feels sorry for Snape. That is plain creepy. My faves are a tie between Harry Potter and Hermione Granger and I do feel sorry for Hagrid because he is so big and dumb. I am very tiny and very smart so I know how it feels to be different too. Although owning a hippogriff would be extremely cool so I don't feel that sorry for him. I did not tell her I have also read all of the Twilight series. Twice. I 'borrowed' them from Fern, who was like soooo Team Jacob but seriously … wrong! Team Edward. Yes!!! Book four was just weird.

For a while it was only Nimmy and me. Awkward. She looked at me and smiled and I looked at her and smiled. This was encouraging, so I told her that her garden was looking awesome. Grandad's cake tasted awesome. And that Dad and Mum have been married for twenty-five years and were in Hong Kong, which was genuinely awesome. She nodded and dozed off and so I kind of said to myself, 'Oh and I found a piece of finger in a tin in the Rosy Room,' and she opened her eyes and said, 'Is it still fresh? How is my darling? Does she miss me? I miss her terribly.' And then she started to cry just little tears, nothing dramatic. I tried very hard not to cry because I must be strong for Grandad. But really underneath I was like … freak-out … Nimmy knows about the finger. What is up with that! MIND. BLOWN!

Then Grandad came back with two pairs of enormous bloomers with 'Lucy Griffin' written on them in HUGE LETTERS in black permanent marker. But by then Nimmy had gone to sleep, and so GG tucked them into her drawer and we left. Normally when we leave she asks GG to please take her with him. She always, always asks to go home. Even if she does not remember Grandad, she seems to remember she is not at her own home. So poor GG always has to think of some nice white lie, like the plumber is coming in the morning and there will be a frightful mess or it is raining too hard to wheel you home — wouldn't want your lovely hair set to frizz etc etc. So it is good she was asleep. GG gave her a kiss and said, 'A good evening to you, Miss Lucy,' and then I started to cry because he always says that and I was touched and saddened and happy all at once. And GG understands.

After tea, Grandad and I started a new holiday book. This holiday book is called *Playing Beatie Bow* and Grandad had chosen it. It was a very good choice and it showed he can see I am growing up. It also reminded me that he is not boring but really a kindred spirit because the book is a bit magical as well. So we took turns to read it out loud and then we went to bed.

When I could hear GG snoring from his room off the front door entrance, I got up and brought the chocolate tin into my bedroom. Then I felt uneasy so I put it under my bed, and then I felt scared so I put it back in the Rosy Room. As I turned to flick off the light switch, I noticed that the big mirror under a sheet seemed to vibrate. Sometimes this happens because the house does need restumping and when the buses go past things do shake. This is what I told myself all the way back to my room, *it's just a bus … just a bus … or a truck or a bus but probably a truck*. But right now it's three-thirty in the morning, I am still awake with the light on and reading *The Philosopher's Stone* again for a bit of light comfort reading. Harry has just met Ron and Hermione. Jealous.

Four

GG has gone to play bridge at his bridge club. Bridge is a tedious card game. Grown-ups can be dull beyond words. But I suppose it is good for him to mix with people his own age like I am supposed to. There is an incredibly rude and smelly old lady he calls Ms HB who lives down the street, and sometimes she knocks on the door and wants to walk with GG to bridge. When this happens he puts his finger on his lips and looks at me with big eyebrows. Then we have to bend down so we are under the front room window and she can't see us. I think he is a bit scared of Ms HB.

The Bridge Hall is four streets away so Grandad

said I could stay here and watch ABC3 for a bit of company. So I said that would be great and turned on the telly and laughed my head off at Scotty Tweedie. He is ADORABLE … according to Fern, not me! I do not like the prank part. I think a lot of them are mean.

When I heard the front gate latch click, I turned off the telly and went to the Rosy Room. I had to calm myself because I am prone to get into a highly suggestible state. I am not sure what this means but I heard Dad telling Mum this, and also that I am 'very sensitive' and 'can get carried away' and yet again a suggestion I should play netball or something vomitous like that. Just because they can't read and listen in at the same time does not mean I can't. It is not a gift. It is a skill I have to practise.

I decided I would set up my laptop to record my investigative findings and then I would replay and freeze-frame it to unearth stuff that I missed in real time. Dad and Linden are always shouting at the TV for a replay and then they slow the footage right down and argue about where an almond-shaped ball is and where it should be. Even though they are shouting, they seem to be very happy at the same time. Bizarre!

I fetched the key, which is a heavy old vintage key that leaves orange rust all over your hands. YUK! I tried to open the door but I didn't have enough hands so I had to put the laptop on the ground. At first I couldn't get the key to move the lock but I jiggled it a little and it opened with a creak. The Rosy Room was very dark. The curtains were heavy and dusty. The room felt different without GG around in the house. So I opened the curtains up to give me a bit of light and courage.

I was totally drawn to the mirror that was under a dusty sheet and wondered what secrets could lie beneath. The sheet was no longer white — it was a powdery grey and had enormous spider webs dangling off it in every direction. I couldn't see any spiders and I examined the webs for ages to be sure. There were dancing dust motes catching the light leading to the mirror. It was totally screaming *dark and mysterious* at me. I was excited but frightened which is an extremely awesome feeling, so I grabbed the sheet and pulled it off like I was a crazy bullfighter swirling a red cape, but I started to cough and my nose is still dripping. Annoying MUCH? The base and frame are made of really cool timber and the mirror is old with black bits where the special mirror paint has worn off. It is a very nice piece of furniture … if you like the haunted Gothic vibe. But it is not a portal to the stylish royal vampire boarding school I thought it might be. This is a shame and a relief. I have to say I am secretly pleased, as the closer I get to the *dark and mysterious* the more scared I feel. This is very tiring.

So emboldened (fab new word), I ripped the sheets off all the furniture to reveal two old wingback chairs and a footstool. There was also a sewing machine that sits in its own desk! There were piles of boxes and cake tins and chocolate tins everywhere. I remembered I had left my laptop on the floor outside but instead of fetching it, I worked out where it should sit for a fabulous panoramic view of all the retro treasures. I felt sad that it is highly plausible Nimmy was/is a crazy hoarder lady and there is enough stuff in here for a whole television show.

Then I had an idea. If there is a finger in one tin,

there might be a toe or a nose in the others. There could be a whole person in this room cut into little tiny pieces and stored in these tins. I felt compelled to open up a shoebox but all I found were postcards dated long ago.

> *Dearest Beryl,* *3/6/1942*
> *One has not lived until one sees 'the changing of the guard' at Buckingham Palace.*

And so on and so forth.

And so my investigation will look at these primary resources first. I feel there could be some revealing background information.

Ten minutes later …

So this is beyond weird and all my life's reading and preparation did not prepare me very well because when it happened I screamed my lungs out and had to run into the kitchen where I still am. It was not very Hermione of me but then she is actually in a magical castle and she knows she is in a magical castle whereas I'm at Grandad's who thinks figs are magic. And I am spewing because I bolted out of the room and accidentally stomped on my laptop. It still works but I have cracked the screen and Dad is going to be furious and will say stuff like, 'Stop daydreaming, Lily, and be more observant of your surroundings.' Thank goodness he is out of the country. I have NO footage to play or replay or freeze and I need it because I want to know if I am in one of my states or in the middle of a supernatural encounter. YIKES!

So this is what happened … I was reading another letter to Beryl, regarding her 'exquisite petunia border garden', when I HEARD A VOICE.

It was a girl's voice. She did not sound very nice. She said, 'Who are you, Chinese child? Do you speak English?' which, in my opinion, is very rude and bordering on being racist. I could not see anyone and I presume she is a ghost. A rude ghost who will not even show herself. So I've been thinking about this and I have decided to go back and confront her.

I would like to shout, 'Show yourself, you plausibly Caucasian child.' But I know I won't. I have calmed down now and I only have a half an hour before Grandad comes home.

And now I have to do my deep breathing and 'think about things rationally'. Am I in one of my highly suggestible states in which my brain is making up stuff? Like the dancing Bratz doll performance of 2011 where I could have sworn Cloe strutted her stuff across my bedroom floorboards. Maybe the voice is a bird twittering in the background, perhaps even a well-trained parrot.

This thought has calmed me down, except now I am thinking about talking parrots that spy on people. A vivid imagination can be a terrible burden.

It is not my imagination … I have heard the rattling again and I KNOW the number 44 bus is not due for twenty minutes. And I heard the VOICE AGAIN and it said, 'Well? Who are you?' The voice was quite demanding and bossy. But then it got softer and nicer, 'Has the house been sold? Do you know where Lucy is? It's been simply ages since I last saw her and she was wearing a tea cosy instead of her hat. 'Twas odd even for Lucy. Is Lucy … Is Lucy dead?'

I knew the answer to this one and I couldn't help but shout back, 'NO!'

My helping instinct kicked in, like ka-chow!

'I saw her yesterday but she is —' I stopped because I didn't know what to say. 'Gone' was hanging around in my brain but I pushed it away.

'What is wrong with her?' the voice screeched. How rude!

Then I had an inspiration. 'She is not herself,' I replied, which ticked all the boxes nicely.

The voice seemed to understand this as she asked, 'Has she taken to her bed again?' I wanted to answer NO but then remembered that Nimmy did spend a lot of time in an easy chair with her head slumped and her mouth open. Was this the same thing?

So I just said, 'She is in a Home.'

And then the voice got very small and a bit scared and it said, 'I don't understand, this is her home … our home. Please, please come and sit with me.'

The girl sounded lonely. I know lonely, it is my specialty subject.

I have decided I will go back into the Rosy Room but I have to push away the thought that she might be an evil sorceress who wants my pinkie finger for a powerful antisocial spell. I am trying to visualise Nimmy's hands and I can count ten fingers and a wedding band and an enormous emerald ring in the shape of a sunflower. It swivels like crazy now. Her hands are as gnarled as the non-magical rosebushes. The random finger is still in the tin. I hope this girl has not come to reclaim it. SCARY! I have had another thought; she could be invisible and watching me right now. NOWHERE IS SAFE! FREAK OUT! I must go in and 'face my fears' just like Dad is always saying. He also says I should have a backup plan/ strategy. If there truly is an evil entity, my plan is to run screaming along the four streets to the bridge club. Be back soon. I hope!

SO MUCH TO TELL …

So I proceeded with caution and terror into the Rosy Room and I saw NOTHING! I looked up at the rose cornices and for a second I thought it was a trick after all, involving a diabolical invisibility cloak. I was about to run from the room when the voice shouted (rude!) at me.

'I'M IN THE MIRROR, YOU SILLY GIRL.'

And there she was! The girl was taller than me but not much. She had curly golden hair and extremely pretty blue eyes. She was wearing what GG would refer to as a 'cotton frock'.

So, no heavy black eye makeup and black supernatural shimmery lace gown.

She looked older than me — like thirteen or something like that.

The first thing I said was, 'Are you a ghost?'

And she laughed as she replied, 'I wish!' This struck me as weird. Her face got all thoughtful and she said, 'I'm not sure what I am anymore.'

Very weird.

I said, 'My dad says there are no such things as ghosts.'

Of course I totally believe in ghosts but listening to my dad's boring voice inside of my head made me feel braver.

'There is so! One used to live in this very room and we frightened him away.' The girl shook her clenched fist fiercely, 'We don't put up with any tommyrot round here.'

Perhaps I should have started with, 'My name is Lily,' but I am not good at this sort of stuff. People stuff. So I tried again and said, 'My name is Lily.'

And the girl looked at me and squealed back, 'My name is Lily too and I remember you.'

FREAKED OUT! … OFFICIALLY!

Then I heard the key in the front door lock and GG was saying, 'Lily Pilly, absolutely cracking game today! Ms HB was ill. Let me freshen up and we will head off to visit Nimmy.'

Then my unidentical, very surprising doppelganger whispered, 'Is that Colin?'

Colin, who in the world is Colin? Then I remembered GG's name is Colin and so I whispered back, 'Yes!'

'Lucy always left me when Colin came home, apparently he is a dreamboat and a real charmer. You'd better go ... Colin is not in on it. Put the dust cover back on and when you can talk again, take it off — that was Lucy's secret signal for me.'

Then the Other Lily stepped back and I couldn't see her anymore until she jumped forward and whisper-shouted, 'DO NOT, UNDER ANY CIRCUMSTANCE, TOUCH THE GLASS!' So I carefully tossed the sheet over the mirror, which was difficult because I am short and even though I 'need to be logical' more often and can be 'overly emotional', I am not so illogical that I want to be stuck in a mirror!

Just then GG (AKA dreamboat Colin!!) popped his head in and said, 'Gracious, you are not in here? Come on, out you come. It's freezing and I need help with my cake.' This is Grandad code for 'stop being weird'. I looked at his long bony nose full of nasal hair and I studied the way he still styles his hair in a part on the side, like there is still enough hair to part. He is quite charming. He never says 'stop daydreaming' or 'don't be silly, Lily'. Instead, he says something like, 'let's go for a little walk around the tulips', which means let's talk of something else for a while.

So I came out of the room.

Five

When we saw Nimmy later that day, it was the first time I really thought she was 'gone'. I do not like the feeling at all. Her eyes were bloodshot and her head was cocked to the side like she was listening to music but there wasn't any music playing. I felt sad like never before. I was sad for Nimmy because she is not Lucy anymore, and I was sad for Other Lily and how all her secrets are wrapped up in this little wispy white-haired head, and how they will never be revealed to me. I tried very hard to 'think of a positive'. At last, I thought perhaps it is a wonderful and magical place inside Nimmy's head and it is much better in her brain than watching telly and looking at the other old farts. So I will rename 'gone' to 'Nimmy Land'. When I daydream, Mum and Dad say, 'Lily's off in Lily Land again!' I am very nice because I do not reply and I only think, *Well it's better than being stuck here in Pig Boy's world.*

As we were walking home, GG took my hand and said, 'Maybe you could visit Isabella tomorrow when I visit Nimmy.' Apparently she is a girl 'round your age' with allegedly 'common interests'. She has just moved next door to GG. It's not her fault that I do not want to meet her. But I do not.

I said, 'No way, José.'

GG sighed and I thought he was going to say 'it's tulip walking time' but he didn't. He sighed again and said, 'Okay, Lily Pilly dear.'

That night we read twenty-three pages of *Playing Beatie Bow* and then we went to bed. I had every intention of chatting with Other Lily but I was so tired from being freaked that I slept all night and woke up in the morning to the smell of figgy goodness (alleged goodness) wafting down the passage.

Grandad was sitting at the top of the table with his black-rimmed spectacles slipping down his nose as he read the paper. He looked up at me and I could tell he had something to tell me that I wouldn't like one little bit. Sheepishly, he peered through his incredibly thick glasses. (Manuel has a sheepish grin … apparently!)

'There seems to be a problem back at your house.'

And before he said anything more I knew that that problem was named Linden.

'What has he done this time?' I said and I got a vibe of what could be coming next. It was an utterly shocking vibe and, as it turned out, my vibe was shockingly correct.

Grandad started off carefully with, 'As it so happens, Linden had a little gathering with some chums.' (Read — evil cronies.)

'And they ended up spray-painting the three

white Turkish Angora cats in Fern's care with her red craft spray-paint. She left it on the kitchen sink so it would be handy for when she had time to finish off her new mural.' (Well, it's not that new, she started it six months ago after she broke up with her boyfriend Cody. Traumatic! It is called *Love Is Only a Figment*.)

Grandad continued, 'Now she has three expensive cats that all look like they have been cleaved open with an axe. Apparently, Linden pleaded it was in the interest of animal welfare as now they cannot be made into hats.' GG had his genuinely cross look on and I was glad. Everyone else thinks Linden is a prankster and that he is hilarious. He is NOT.

As if the cats were ever going to be made into hats. Ridiculous and completely erroneous! It has taken me a long time to be able to use *erroneous* in a sentence because it is a Linden-ism … a very mean Linden-ism. (In our family when someone says the same word a lot, my dad calls it their 'ism'. This means it is one of their catchphrases. Poor Dad doesn't realise he has the most 'isms' of all. He can be a bit repetitive in a nice but slightly boring logical way.)

When I was eight, Linden would say to me, 'You are so erroneous!' like I was clever and pretty. He would say, 'Wow, that assignment on Adélie penguins was way erroneous, well done,' and then he went as far as to say my birth was a most erroneous affair, like I was Aurora from *Sleeping Beauty*. This went on for weeks. I began to get suspicious about the word's meaning and its nastiness was confirmed when I overheard Dad on the phone telling another guy his calculations were erroneous and they did not want any MISTAKES for the client. Then I looked up the meaning in the dictionary and felt sick.

So I dobbed on him to Mum and she was way … WAY angry. Angry big-time! Linden got grounded for a whole month and has hated my guts ever since because he missed a big party that gazillions of his friends were going to. I felt a bit bad because I didn't really want him to miss the party — Linden out of the house is always the best kind of Linden. But he still hates me and perhaps this is why I am having such supernatural luck — because I have a real live enemy. He makes Draco Malfoy look like a doofus.

Fern phoned Dad who phoned Grandad, who very kindly said it was all right if Linden caught the bus down to us for the last week of the holidays. This is one of the main problems with the charming Colin. He is too TOO NICE. I am not a baby but I burst into tears and without thinking I ran straight to the Rosy Room. For once the key turned straight away and I flung open the door. Dramatically. I threw myself into one of the cold old chairs and then … I might have got a teensy-weensy bit carried away with my crying because I started to hyperventilate until I felt woozy. The mirror started to rattle, but then Grandad came in with a cup of hot chocolate and a paper bag, so it stopped. He spoke to me in a soothing voice and actually said he would SPEAK to LINDEN about his BEHAVIOUR. This made me feel much better but certainly not my normal self.

Grandad did not visit Nimmy today. He said that he had a little cold but I never saw him sniff or cough once — but he did mention Nimmy was a bit susceptible to bugs at the mo. He did have a longer nap, which allowed me more time in the Rosy Room, but I think he stayed home because I got overwrought and he was worried about me. BLESS!

When I pulled back the sheet today, Other Lily was waiting for me. She had a very caring look on her face and the first thing she said was, 'How are you now, dear?' which was very nice of her. I was not ready to talk about the Linden thing so I said breezily (fab new word) that I was super. She didn't believe me but she was quiet about the tears. I guess girls in mirrors can be quite sympathetic and intuitive too.

I had some questions to ask her, mostly about the finger, her entrapment plus I wanted to know who Mock Cream Beryl was.

So I opened up the chocolate box and pulled out the finger and I showed it to her. I was expecting her to be curious or disgusted but she actually clapped her hands together with glee and did a very pretty dance. 'You found it! You found it!' she shouted and I had to say, 'Inside voices, Lily, we don't want to freak out Col,' and she laughed even harder.

Once she had settled down with her barely contained joy, she told me that Lucy had lost it and that they had spent YEARS looking for it. I said I was glad I found it for them but what was the deal with it anyway. Other Lily held up her hand in the glass and I could instantly see she had a finger missing. The finger belongs to Other Lily! Then, get this, she started laughing and put her foot up and there was a piece missing from the sandal and the tip of her toe was gone!

GROSS-A-ROONEY!

'Haven't found my tippy-toe have you?' she asked. I said no but I would start looking.

She watched me for a moment and asked, 'How is Colin these days?' I replied he is fabulous and the best grandad in the world.

Other Lily smiled and said, 'Lucy loves him dearly too … what is a Home like?' I told her it's not as nice as it sounds.

'Is Lucy's favourite colour still emerald green?' I answered yes it was.

'Does she still sing like a bird?' I said no and I then asked a question next. 'How do you know Colin and Lucy anyway?'

Other Lily laughed again and I have to say that her cheerful chuckle was getting on my nerves a bit. She said, 'Lucy is my twin sister, silly billy. She is the eldest by eight minutes and thirty-two seconds.'

I have to say that I was surprised, as in blown away, as in gobsmacked, because there has never been any mention of ANY sister let alone a TWIN one. The thought floated through my head that she was indeed an evil witch and she was making up porky pies but then I remembered the picture of two girls in cotton frocks. One was holding a cat and the other was patting it. So there could be some sort of truth to it and I have made a mental note to ask GG in a roundabout non-confrontational (Fern's word) sort of way. What else don't I know about this family?

I really wanted to ask her how she came to be trapped in the mirror but I felt like the answer was obvious to her. It was certainly not obvious to me but I did not want to be called a 'silly billy' again.

So I kept looking for the toe tip by opening up all the tins and shoeboxes and stuff. Another one of Beryl's riveting letters fell out and this time she had the secret to a crisp and moist lamington and before I could stop myself I said, 'Who is Beryl?'

This caught Other Lily unawares because she answered, 'My mama, of course,' in a very quiet voice and her eyes fell to the other wingback chair, which has a small knitted rug folded, resting on the cushion. I looked into the mirror and I could see tiny tears running down her pretty chin. I am beyond BLUE for her just remembering it now.

And then I just had to ask, 'What happened? Why are you inside a mirror?'

Other Lily looked sad and a bit troubled. It was the sort of look my mum gets when she has been thinking for a long time about a problem that she doesn't have the answer to. I hope she is thinking, 'Why do I have one awesome child, two normal children and one that is an odious Pig Boy named Linden.'

Six

Other Lily (OL for short, it's called an *initialism*!) opened her mouth just as I had one of my on-the-spot light-bulb moments. I shouted, 'Shazam! Hang on just a mo,' and ran into my bedroom to get my slightly smashed laptop.

I returned to the Rosy Room, opened up the computer to face the mirror and then I hit record. Lucy was totally intrigued by it and I had to explain it was like a typewriter that could make movies and access all kinds of books, pictures, music and information across the *whole wide world*. I showed her my amazing ebook collection. She loved the adult Harry Potter covers — she got their symbolism straight away.

OL was impressed with the laptop and said (which I thought was way clever) that it was like Lucy's old typewriter and gramophone together with all her records, her mum Beryl's entire newspaper hoard and top-secret recipe notepads, her dad Ken's home projector, family slides and the wireless radio PLUS her own entire book/encyclopedia collection and Kodak Brownie camera all rolled into one. OL said she had never seen anything like it 'in all her born days'. She absolutely loved it and even hinted she was a teensy-weensy bit envious. It was like her nine fingers yearned to touch the keyboard.

I showed her a few more things it could do and I took a photo of her and turned it into pop art. Fern is so into pop art and she is always changing things to look either cutting-edge or retro. I am not sure which one pop art is. OL asked me if I could get her an ebook of *Alice in Wonderland* as Lucy had lost theirs. She had so enjoyed listening to Lucy read it day after day. She never got tired of it. I said Colin didn't have an internet connection so I was sorry but I couldn't. I have not read *Alice in Wonderland* but I did not like the movie so I was not *that* sorry.

OL kept asking me all kinds of questions about the laptop and it was almost like she didn't want to talk about how she got stuck in the mirror and I could understand … but I was also dying to know so I said, 'Why don't we make a movie of you telling the story of how you got stuck in the mirror.' I am clever too.

First of all OL patted down her adorable curls and smiled sheepishly but then she took a deep breath, slid down to the ground and sat crossed-legged. She played with her cotton skirt and kept smoothing out all the wrinkles over and over again. I know that feeling — it is stressed to the max. So I said, 'Don't worry, we can listen to music if you like, or I could read Harry Potter to you,' but I was sooo hoping she would tell her story.

Finally, she whispered, 'Do you remember when we first met … I mentioned a ghost?'

I shut my eyes like I was trying hard to remember and said, 'Yeah … kind of.'

I did not want to tell her that evening I had an 'accident of an embarrassing nature'. GG had my favourite PJs dry and extra fluffy for me the next day.

'As you know, this house is terribly old. There really was a ghost — and his name was Edgar. He made himself known to Lucy and I five months and three days before our fourteenth birthday. We had been living in the house for nearly a year. Fabian, our cat, had sensed him straight away and became uncharacteristically skittish. Edgar had been here all along but our 'spiritual energy' was not in the least bit powerful or interesting until then. He also said Ken and Beryl were the dullest people in the entire universe; living or dead.'

'How terrifying … and rude!' I whispered while crossing my legs and sitting down as well.

'Oh, not really, he was more of a nuisance than anything else. Lucy and I called him Edgar the Pudding Head. You see, Lucy could see him and his enormous grinning face. I couldn't. But that didn't matter because Edgar was one of those show-off poltergeists — always banging and moving our things around. He was wily enough to only put on a show in front of Lucy and myself. He loved to provoke me on purpose because I suppose I am quite orderly and tidy.'

She sighed and looked around at the scattered topsy-turvy piles of top quality jumble. 'He thought he was hilarious but he was not! Edgar had just turned fourteen when he died — apparently he had choked to death in 1898 in a pie stuffing competition. He was the outright winner but unable to claim his prize on account of being dead. The highly desired prize was a bar of Cadbury chocolate from the homeland and it went to the runner-up who had had the commonsense not to inhale the pastry up his nose. This riled Edgar beyond belief and he spent the rest of his afterlife utterly fixated on sweet treats. He was forever ruining Mama's prize-winning cakes, and Lucy and I would get the blame! And the punishment! OUTRAGEOUS!' Other Lily's blue eyes sparked and glowered.

Naturally concerned, I asked, 'What kind of punishment?'

'Why, the wooden spoon to the derrière of course!'

'Beryl, you are outrageous!' I shouted, but OL seemed not to be worried at all by her mama's actions … like a wallop to the tooshie was totally acceptable. Shudder! Thank goodness our house is a spank-free zone!

I do not like Beryl.

'We muddled on, the three of us — sometimes Edgar was quiet for ages and ages, other times he was chatty and cheeky and then patty cakes, devils-on-horseback and lamingtons would fly around the kitchen. Lucy would laugh and clap her hands in delight but I was furious … it was a waste of good food AND a paddywhack for us. Lucy said the smack was worth the spectacle of it all. She could be very bold, you know, but I suppose she could see Edgar and talk to him while I kept my nose in a book and tried hard not to pay him any attention — he seemed to thrive on it. I suppose I was a little bit jealous. Anyway, after a few long chats with Lucy, Edgar settled down in this room because it was off the kitchen and he could smell all of Mama's delicious cooking. He even stopped juggling treats around. And things were fine for a time but then —'

Other Lily stopped talking and played with her skirt some more and then fiddled with her sandal strap so I looked at her foot — and saw the spot where her toe used to live! I tried hard not to look at the missing chunk. Plus I desperately wanted to ask what kind of a treat was a devil-on-horseback!*

'It's all my fault,' she whispered in a voice I knew was hurting her throat to keep the tears in. Heartbreaking.

'You see, Lucy and I always shared a room. Always … and we were so lucky because as well as being sisters, we were jolly good friends. But then we got out of sorts and I became pernickety. I was jealous of her little tête-à-têtes with Edgar. On the rare occasion that Edgar would hear Lucy playing tunes on her gramophone, he would float on into our bedroom at night and together they would dance to a silly crooning man called Frank Sinatra, and Lucy would twirl and strut and shake her derrière. I was scandalised … it was almost like she was enjoying herself … dancing with a boy! A dead boy, no less. It was very vexing. There was one song I remember well, it was called "I've Got a Crush on You" and I knew nothing good would come from her shenanigans. When I look back on it, which I must confess I often do, I now realise she was simply appreciating the music and the movement of it all. But at the time … some nasty words may have flown out of my mouth.'

OL looked up and saw my eyes pop and my wide-open mouth shout dismay at her without words.

'Oh don't worry, Lucy could be quite feisty as well. When I wanted to read at night, she would want to sleep and then snap the light off … just like that — SNAP! When I wanted to sleep, of course Lucy would insist on having the lamp on so she could draw the supposedly dreamy Frank Sinatra in pencil. This went on and on and caused quite a few more cross words and bad tempers, until Papa had a very good idea. He suggested I move into the room off the kitchen just before Christmas as a reward for all my hard work and good grades! I was his favourite little bookworm, he said, and Lucy was his favourite little chanteuse, and we were different but equally adorable.'

I like Ken.

Her story was epically intense and even now when I play it back, my heart hurts for Other Lily. But I am torn — it was incredibly rude of Lucy not to let Other Lily read but as for being able to see AND dance with a spectre, that's AWESOME. I'm basically in awe that my actual grandmother is a medium and it is highly plausible that by the time I turn thirteen I could have this gift too. SCARY WONDERFUL!!

Then OL went on to reveal the most incredible story, now that I'm her *confidante* (a French word that means she trusts me with her secrets).

It was nearly Christmas time. Other Lily and Lucy were buzzing with sheer happiness as they knew their mama, Beryl, was working hard sewing new matching dresses AND had crocheted them each an identical new bedspread in quite a cutting-edge fancy 1940s pattern to celebrate their individuality. Bless! Ken papered the walls in this rosy spewalicious wallpaper that is still here today. Apparently Ken's catchphrase was, 'If it's a job worth doing, it's worth doing well.'

Beryl helped choose (read — fully chose) the wallpaper.

One fateful Saturday morning, Ken got Beryl off her Singer sewing machine to help him move Lily's mirror into the newly minted Rosy Room. This is where it all went wrong. BIG-TIME!

Ken didn't realise they had 'a poltergeist with an insatiable appetite for sugary tidbits residing there already' (OL is a total word nerd too) and when they moved her mirror into the room, Edgar quickly shunted it back out into the hallway with a twirl and a kick. Poor Fabian ran outside screeching and hissing and hid under the house for hours.

Ken's mind was blown AWAY! This was when Kenneth P. Dunnings of *Dunnings Hardware and Nursery* passed out cold, hitting his head with a thwack on the freshly polished floorboards. Apparently he was a sensible man and flying furniture was too much for all of his senses — but mostly his sense of sight.

Of course OL knew it was troublemaker Edgar and she was ENRAGED. She pointed her finger at the mirror and screeched that it was time to leave and he was to pack his pudding-filled bags and to go AT ONCE.

OL's boldness caught Edgar off guard and he must have overshot his dramatic exit through the wall as he ended up in the bathroom with Lucy, who was in a state of undress and ONLY had on her trainer brassiere plus a singlet tucked into her sport bloomers which were pulled up over her knickers with matching anklet cuff socks. 'Practically naked!' was how OL described it.

It was Lucy's turn to get all fired up as she rushed out of the bathroom to find her pa on the ground quite 'insensible'.

'EDGAR!' she shouted and apparently also pointed her finger — and because Lucy could see him, it really hit the mark. 'Edgar, I explained to you that Lily is going to have your room because she is driving me mad with her neat-as-a-pin attitude and incessant blasted studying.'

'Language, Lucy!' warned Beryl, who was obviously upset about the ruckus but held that rules were rules.

I really do not like Beryl.

It was at this point of her recount that Other Lily started to cry and her bottom lip became beyond wobbly. She held her breath as a tiny river of tears trickled down her nose. She said Lucy's words had cut her to the very core and she looked at her with pleading eyes. But Edgar seized the moment to say Lily was driving him mad too and perhaps HE should move into Lucy's room so they could dance and eat cake to their heart's content and — BANG — Lucy's gramophone cranked up and Ol' Blue Eyes Frankie was singing 'I've Got a Crush on You'. DRAMA!

Lucy quickly realised what she had just said and freaked. Lucy did not want to share her room with an amorous pudding and cried out, 'I am sorry, Lily.'

Edgar, although greedy, was no fool. He quickly worked out that he was on the losing team and pleaded that he might be allowed to stay in the washhouse where he had 'formerly resided since 1898 without any bother'. But Lucy said NO and asked him in no uncertain terms to leave and never come back.

Other Lily got on the bandwagon and shouted,

'Just BUZZ OFF, Edgar!'

Edgar looked at Lucy, who was like … hopping mad, and then he looked at Lily who was like … smiling a 'take that, scallywag' smirk. Furious, he began to chant in a singsong voice:

SILLY LILY, DON'T DILLY DALLY
INTO THE MIRROR YOU GO
SILLY LILY, DON'T DILLY DALLY
STAY THERE AND NEVER GROW

He PUSHED Lily into the mirror. Lucy said later that evening that Edgar had a look of utter surprise on his face that his chant had actually worked, but then his eyes quickly narrowed and you could see he was thinking that this was a very good solution to their little accommodation problem.

Other Lily ran hard at the mirror to get back out, hands outstretched, but when she touched the glass her finger exploded and fell right into Lucy's hand. (Impressive Nimmy — I would have dropped it for sure.)

Lucy screamed and screamed and screamed. She yelled, 'Give her back to me, you rotten scoundrel!' and went to beat the glass with her fists, but Mock Cream Beryl had the presence of mind to stop her by wrestling her to the ground. From the freshly polished floorboards they beseeched Edgar to 'GET LILY OUT THIS INSTANT!'

But Edgar rallied and puffed up 'like he was the peacock with the trump card' (OL is also great at similes) and said with authority, 'Please say we can be friends again.'

'Yes, of course, Edgar,' shouted back Lucy in a state of despair.

Edgar tried to undo his curse and went through all combinations of words and melodies — but nothing happened. Over and over he repeated the words but this did not break the spell, it seemed to only make it stronger and sparks flared around the hall and off into the kitchen. Beryl's perfect pavlova was practically glowing green!

Frightened, he turned to Lucy and said, 'Say I can stay in the room off the kitchen and we can be the best of friends,' but Edgar's courage was failing and he was totally confused — 'Silly sausage? Pilly Polly? Oh pooh … please say I can stay. Say it, say it.'

Stunned, Lucy — who was prone to high emotion — shouted, 'I will never ever be your friend again!'

Then something happened that no one expected but that would have *dire consequences* for a very long time. Edgar began to explode into tiny colourful shards of light whilst emitting the most delicious scent. He looked down at his dissolving self and then back at Lily while mumbling the spell one more time in an overwrought voice. As he faded away he whispered, 'Sorry, dear girls ...' and then disappeared forever. Lucy had broken his non-beating heart.

Here OL finished her story and I was sniffling A LOT because it was very sad indeed.

'And I have been trapped ever since. After years of reflection — forgive the pun — I am not sure what I am anymore.' OL closed her eyes, covered her face and breathed deeply for a mo.

I was totally devastated and I shut the laptop. I didn't need to replay or freeze-frame. I will never forget this story ever. It is imprinted on my brain.

Other Lily now drew her knees up to her chin, put her arms over her head and was silent. Then the silence got awkward and my brain was overloaded with questions like 'don't you ever get hungry or tired or gassy?'

It was like OL had read my mind because she looked up and said, 'I don't sleep, I don't need food, I don't get cold and I don't feel a thing except boredom, loneliness and … regret … it's the most terrible feeling — rather like indigestion. I'm sorry for being a sourpuss and a grumblepot.'

After a long time in silence, she sighed deeply and said, 'Lately I am beginning to feel like I am losing my stuffing. I feel like flat lemonade … not a bubble or a zing left some days.'

As the words left her mouth she turned sideways and, just for a moment, she disappeared out of my sight. She swung back round to face me and there she was again, all pretty and polished. Then she turned to her other side to try to catch a glance of the sunlight sneaking into the hallway. She said she loved the patterns dancing on the boards.

It happened again.

I literally could not see her. She was like my well-loved bookmark. She was FLAT.

Is this normal behaviour for mirror girls or is OL changing?

So confusing.

Vexation City.

*According to Beryl's notes, a 'devil-on-horseback' is a tasty morsel of dried fruit wrapped snuggly in a lardy piece of bacon. It is not an apocalyptic horseman.

Seven

I found I was craving bacon so I made myself a bacon sandwich before I went back to the Rosy Room to check on Other Lily. After such an intense story I was worried she might have literally evaporated into nothing. She was so weak! But she was there as always waiting for me and she had more to share.

A LOT more!

The hours that followed Other Lily's disappearance into the mirror were a terrible time for the Dunnings. Beryl had been struck dumb for a time but then went into a very loud state of conniption. She bellowed for the doctor, the police and the reverend. Ken came round and saw his Lily in the mirror, hit a high note there for a moment or two and then fainted away again. When Other Lily saw her parents so upset, she kicked her side of the mirror hard and her toe blew off. This gave them all an even greater fright. Beryl insisted she should not touch the glass ever again. As Beryl was saying this, Lucy went and touched the glass really softly. Her fingerprints were wiped clean off and it hurt her so much she started screaming again. Young Nimmy became totally unhinged but I suppose if I saw one of my sisters in the mirror I would go crazy too. If I saw Linden I would throw a party — IN FRONT OF HIM — with a DJ and a slushy machine.

When Ken got conscious for the second time, he moved the mirror into the Rosy Room as Beryl said it was creating a clutter in the hallway. She had decided she did not want anyone to know about the strange goings-on. Just like that! Fate sealed. Ken wanted tea and cake first to get his thoughts together but Beryl said NO. *No discussion to be entered into, Kenneth.* Beryl was prone to saying this a lot.

Then, a knock at the door. Ken hit the ground

once more, weakened by the exertion and lack of sugar. Thud! Total panic station! A small charming voice cried out, 'Is everything all right?' and Beryl (who believed in manners) opened the door. There stood Miss Janet Knoblett, the girls' beloved teacher who had brought books for Lily, records for Lucy and chocolates for Beryl.

Even though Mock Cream Beryl was a large lady, she could not hide her flaked-out husband lying face down in the hallway. Miss Knoblett (who was a kindred spirit and excellent at reading vibes) saw him and the look on Beryl and Lucy's faces and knew *something of a significant nature had just taken place.*

'It's Lily,' shouted Lucy.

And Beryl had the presence of mind to say, 'She is missing, we can't find her — please alert the sergeant, go … go … go quickly,' and then went back to wailing and shouting and sobbing all at the same time. (She had hiccups for two days.)

Beryl threw the dust cloth over the mirror and shut the door to the Rosy Room when the sergeant arrived. She wanted to keep this a secret. But guilt-ridden Lucy moved all her things into the Rosy Room that very night to be close to her sister. She apologised about being silly over the lamp and for her hurtful comments and told Other Lily she was very insightful regarding Edgar and that the two sisters were never to separate again. Anytime OL got sad or a bit panicky, she knew she could call out to her. OL didn't often cry out for her because Lucy needed all her strength for life on the outside. But just being there for her was a great comfort.

I know this is a paradox (according to Fern, life is full of them!) but listening to lovely stories about a lovely sister REMINDED ME ABOUT LINDEN! SPEW!

Linden is coming here soon and I don't want him to find Other Lily and I don't want him to come at all. FULL STOP!!!!

Other Lily noticed my brow going all intense and furrowed and she said, 'Please, won't you tell me what is wrong?'

I shrugged and said nothing, but seriously, I was slightly jealous that *my* Nimmy was *her* Lucy first and I got stuck with a pig instead of a cool twin sister. Young Lucy sounds like so much fun — not that I am into fun, it's totally overrated. I just bravely shrugged again and said, 'What happened next?'

Other Lily said everyone eventually calmed down and the family got into a pretty cozy routine. Lucy, Beryl and Ken would sit here in this bedroom with her of an evening. So sweet! And they would show her all the new stuff in the world and read her the newspaper and listen to music. Beryl would knit in one old chair and Ken would read his newspaper in the other and on the little stool sat Lucy … sounds pretty comfy. They even finished papering the room in this vomitous rose wallpaper to remind her of the garden. Beryl was 'well pleased' with the result.

Other Lily looked sad and I asked her if she was okay.

'Not too bad considering the circumstances, and much better for having you here,' she answered. So brave!

And then I felt so incredibly sorry for both Nimmy and Other Lily that I started to cry. Again. This must have reminded her of my little performance this morning because she asked me what was wrong back then.

I took a deep breath and said, 'My brother is coming to stay and he hates me.' I must admit, I just kept crying and the tears were very hot and angry and I was embarrassed so MUCH that I kicked over a pile of boxes — and newspaper cuttings, birthday cards and old electricity bills flew everywhere.

'Not Linden the handful?' asked OL.

'Yes!' I said, 'What is up with that? How come you know stuff? Please explain!'

Apparently, Nimmy would bring in all the babies in the family for her sister to see. She started off with her own son, my dad (John), and then he got too big and too aware of stuff, like that aunts shouldn't be in mirrors, and she had to stop. But when Nimmy had grandchildren, she would show her each baby. Each child could visit until they were nearly three. Sometimes she would watch Zinnia and Fern play and it was really lovely and very good for her heart.

'Do you remember me?' I asked, soooo excited.

'Yes,' she said, 'because you were the last. Linden was three and he kept climbing up onto the top of the wooden base, and Lucy was holding newborn you and she kept pulling Linden back by the pants until she had to take him outside so she could show me the new baby. You were utterly, utterly adorable with a tiny little head like a fresh peach … simply the most divine baby of all.'

She said she saw photos of John and Letty and us kids growing up over the years and she knew all kinds of snippets of stories about us. Then Other Lily looked at me and asked, 'Did Letty find her Vietnamese birth mother as she was thinking about doing years ago?'

I answered, 'No.'

Other Lily said this was a shame and I sighed and agreed … only because I want to find out what mysteries could lay there. Then I told OL about Nanna Pinkington, who is Mum's adopted mum but really her true mum as the Universe chose for them to be together. Pinkie (*thanks once again, Zinnia*) is the best mum and nanna in the world. She lives in a unit that is very close to us (which is great) but that's very clean and neat. She likes to give old things away! Not so great! The only mystery surrounding her is her love of *Midsomer Murders* on the television. Actually, this is not strictly true. Not the bit about Nanna Pinkie loving English detectives but the bit about me only being interested in Mum's birth family for its intrigue factor. Last Christmas, I overheard my sisters talking about it too. Fern said she looks Vietnamese but feels ridiculous because she doesn't know a word of the language, and Zinnia said she was sick of her new Spanish friends asking her to whip up a bowl of pho and being surprised when she bakes perfect pumpkin scones. (Nimmy recipe!) Fern and her friends are going to Vietnam before she heads off to Europe and they wanted to visit her ancestral village. She had to tell them she had no idea. Realistically, Treebark is our ancestral village. Fern said it was Mum's decision and we needed to support her and stuff.

OL is awesome at reading vibes, just like I am, because the next thing she said was she was so ashamed of being snippy and tetchy with me at the start … and for calling me 'Chinese girl' when I am actually Australian with Vietnamese heritage.

She often wondered if the house had been sold, because it had been a long time since Lucy had gone away for good. Long before that, her visits had become erratic and sometimes Lucy would forget who she was. Sometimes — this was even worse — Lucy would think SHE was the girl in the mirror and would start to brush HER hair and straighten HER hat. (OL does not even wear a hat!) There were days when Lucy wouldn't visit at all as 'she had taken to her bed because of her nerves' — I suspect it was the neurons not working, which is close enough. GG has explained it to me.

I told OL it had been four years since Lucy had gone into the Home, so about seven years since she had last seen my adorable face. She said she had been so lonely and frightened and bored, but mostly lonely, in the mirror that she thought she was having one of those bad dreams that make you wake up and scream. Except she never quite got round to the wake up and scream bit. She said it made the whole cake-cart-wheeling Edgar episode pale into utter insignificance and she now wished she had let the greedy pudding head stay in his own room and not been such a jolly spoilsport.

Apparently, when Nimmy realised her neurons were on the slide, she suggested that they let Colin in on it (the sister-in-law behind glass deal) and OL was totally up for it but then poor Lucy forgot to mention it to him before it was too late. I actually got a lump in my throat because that is seriously sad.

But OL was like, so positive. She shook herself and shuddered, 'There I go again being as miserable as a bandicoot … so sorry.' Then she smiled her brightest smile and asked, 'Is Linden still a handful?'

'Handful? He is a mental case!' I answered, only because it is the TRUTH.

Eight

I told Other Lily all about Linden and how mean he is to me, including the erroneous story and another one involving my trumpet case being hidden on the school bus by him and his friends, which led me to have a very public panic attack because that trumpet is expensive to Dad and precious to me. One of his friends, named Harry, slid it out from under Linden's seat and said sorry. Linden teased him and said he was a Lily lover pansy.

I even told her about the time Linden held my head under the water at our family Christmas pool party and Zinnia had to hit him hard on the head with the leaf scoop to get him to stop. Meanwhile Fern had dived in and rescued me. I vomited up all my chunky Christmas ham and potato salad and I have to say, throwing up lumpy potato is almost as bad as nearly drowning.

Other Lily was outraged. OUTRAGED. And she shouted, 'He sounds PERFECTLY GHASTLY AND A BULLY AND A RAT AND A FINK TO BOOT!' and she paced back and forth until at last she said, 'To be perfectly frank, he needs to be taught a lesson.'

I really REALLY REALLY like Other Lily. She is the best friend ever!

And then Other Lily smiled, what I can only describe as a wicked smile, and I wondered again if she was an evil fairy. This did not stop me from liking her. It actually increased my like. But she is not, of course, an evil entity of any description. She is just plain awesome. Other Lily bent over to touch her toes like she was in training for the Bully Olympics. She turned to her side and did a few quick knee lifts and suddenly she was flat again. All I could see of her were knobbly knees and swinging arms, like a jerking ribbon. OL was as flat as the Queen on an old postage stamp. She was so busy being chipper that she did not see my open mouth of SHOCK. I pulled myself together.

OL turned and jogged towards me and said she COMPLETELY understands how I feel because when she lived outside the mirror in the real world, there was a girl down the street named Dawn Hornbuckle, who would pull her plaits and set her dog onto her AND the wretched beast had even taken a piece out of her ankle. Other Lily popped her leg up and showed me the scar. It was still quite raw and angry looking. It made the space where the missing toe was on the other leg look healthy and completely normal and acceptable. This is how utterly horrible it is. *Wretched*, a fab new word I learnt from OL.

'It happened a fortnight before I got stuck in here,' she said sadly, 'Mama had just removed the bandages.'

'What happened?' I asked. What bad luck to have a dog bite you and then become trapped in a parallel dimension.

'I was riding my new bicycle past her house

when Deadly Dawn opened the gates and released Chompers — he was a very large and peculiar-smelling Doberman with a deep hatred of shiny bicycles and girls. I suspect it was because Dawn was a cycling girl and I suspect that she terrorised Chompers as much as she terrorised me.'

'How long ago did this happen?' I asked, taking another sneak peek at the scar. Shudder.

'December the 12th, 1947… It feels so long ago. I have lost track of time. When Mama and darling Pa died, Lucy helped me keep track of the days by sneaking in and telling me the time and the day and what the weather was like. She would read bits and bobs from the newspapers and sometimes, if Colin was out at bridge, she would bring in the radio and we could listen to tunes. We even tried a portable television set but we could never get the rabbit-ears antenna to work properly and when the sewing machine was running as well … it was a nightmare!' Other Lily sighed. 'One day, she came in with a tea-cosy on her head and I asked her if she had the morning papers handy — but she couldn't remember what a paper was. I thought she was joking until she started crying and snapped, 'What a darn nuisance this paper thing must be … whatever it was.'

And then we were both quiet for a long time and both felt a bit dreary until I broke the silence by saying how I wished I had a twin sister and not a psycho brother.

OL's eyes began to shine with mischief again and she whispered, 'We will teach him a lesson for sure.'

Just then, Grandad shouted out, 'A certain favourite cake is ready for a certain favourite grandchild.'

'Is it a chocolate ganache and hazelnut cake?' asked OL and I nodded. She said this cake was Lucy's favourite too and the charming Colin would make it for her on the weekends. I feel very special that I have something in common with the beautiful girl that was Nimmy in the photograph but I feel very scared that if I eat too much of it, I will end up like Nimmy in the Home, all jiggly with drooping bits.

I am feeling loved and mysterious all in one.

But I have a voice niggling at me in the back of my

head. I think it might be a kind of logic. Why does Other Lily keep going flat? I am trying not to think about what this means.

Can't stop thinking about it.

What does it mean?

Nine

I have been spending every minute in the Rosy Room with OL and now I feel very sorry for GG, as he must miss me terribly. I told him I was collecting all the old recipes from letters and that I would make a recipe book for him and he said that sounded like a very worthwhile idea and gave me a plastic folder and a label gun. (It's left over from when Nimmy was still at home — everything around here is labelled!) And so I am sorting and looking for a tippy-toe and recipes and secrets of any kind.

I came across a beautiful jam tart box full of blue letters with *Par Avion* on them. They are aerogrammes, which sounds cutting edge, but I think it just means letters written on blue paper and sent by an aeroplane, which is not that radical. On the front are these readymade stamps of the Queen wearing a tiara and she looks as pretty as, maybe even prettier than Kate Middleton.

These letters are from Lucy to Beryl and Ken and Lily. Lucy and Colin went to London and then toured something called the Continent. Lucy describes tulip gardens and old clocks and pointy shoes and twirly spaghetti and Yorkshire puddings and Monte Carlo — which, as it turns out, is a place and not just a tasty biscuit. There are heaps of letters all folded upon themselves. Some of them are boring and some are awesome — complaining about chilblains and asking about Fabian her darling cat all the time … Yawnfest. But describing the midnight sun … Amazeballs.

I shook one of the letters and out popped a photograph of Lucy and Colin in Paris. Colin had his coat over their heads and Lucy was looking at Colin in such a nice way. Colin's hair was dark and wavy and parted in the exact same part he has now (except there is hair in the photo) and he was wearing large black-rimmed specs that are incredibly ugly — poor Colin. You would need to be charming to wear that freaky nerd-alarm on your face. I held up the pic for OL to see and she sighed and said, 'What a jadorable couple.' This is French for totes adorable. And they are.

And that's when I had a very important thought. These little crinkly pieces of blue tissue paper are like Nimmy's memories; it's like looking into the Pensieve with Dumbledore smiling behind me … except behind me is a squashed thirteen-year-old girl trapped in a mirror. These soft petal-like papers are special and amazing and irreplaceable. I looked around the room and there are heaps and heaps of tins and boxes full to the brim with them. It's like all the good thoughts Lucy ever had are written here for Other Lily. They still exist and I can read them. I can see into Nimmy's mind before the dementia came and ate up all the memories like a ticked-off Chompers. I looked up and saw OL smiling kindly at me and realised … she was like a LIVING MEMORY BANK about Lucy and Beryl and Ken and John and Letty and all of us, in a way. I looked like a peach, for heaven's sake. This is IMPORTANT STUFF.

I am borrowing some photos and a couple of letters as they make me feel very close to Other Lily and Lucy in the good old days. My life seems to have happened *after* the good old days because Zinnia and Fern can remember heaps about Nimmy before she went off into Nimmy Land. Linden doesn't care. I can remember some stuff too, like how she could peel potatoes in one long curly piece and how GG would laugh loudly at her jokes. He would bend over and come up with happy tears running off his face. But my sisters have years of memories. Nimmy even met Manuel and got her flirt on with him as she spoke to him in Spanish. She will never meet my future dreamboat and that makes me sad.

Ten

Last night I couldn't sleep and not even reading about Hermione and Viktor Krum hitting the D-floor at the Triwizard Yule Ball helped. I had to come clean with OL and tell her that Nimmy has dementia.

So this morning I did and she said, 'What is this?' So I went and got GG's book on it and read her the description and symptoms and stuff. I left out the PROGNOSIS as my throat was really sore from trying not to blub like a baby but then I did blub like a baby anyway.

When I looked up, Lily was blubbing like a baby too and she cried out, 'It would do my heart the world of good if I could just see my dearest Lucy one more time,' and then I started howling because that is IMPOSSIBLE and I am grateful that GG is a bit deaf and is outside pruning the roses. So we both got ourselves into a bit of a state when GG's big old-fashioned phone rang. I pulled myself together and thought rationally and ran to GG's bedroom and answered it.

It was Linden and he said, 'Are you looking forward to seeing me? Because I will be there tonight at six pm, loser.'

I said, 'Thank you for that information, I will tell GG ASAP.' Then I hung up and ran back to OL and started howling again.

'Who was it, dear?' asked Lily.

'The HANDFUL arrives tonight at six pm,' I replied.

Then we had a secret chat about teaching Linden a lesson. I started to feel a bit better but I knew in my heart that Linden is a bigger handful than Dawn and Chompers Hornbuckle put together.

Other Lily said the key to executing a terrific idea

was in the groundwork.

'Does Linden have any *foibles*?' she asked me.

'He does have a furuncle on the side of his neck that he takes antibiotics for,' I said.

She laughed, 'No, I mean weak character points.'

'I can't think of one,' I said, 'he is much taller and stronger and meaner than me.'

Lily told me to look a little deeper and so I thought hard and answered, 'He is a fussy eater and is a smelly Pig Boy.' I added, 'Oh, and Dad said he is easily stimulated and when I asked Fern what this meant, she said he has the attention span of a gnat.'

Lily thought these were indeed foibles enough and gave her plenty to work with.

Well, Linden is here. He is completely ignoring me in his scowly way, which suits me fine. Being ignored does not leave psychological damage.

I have taken the key and locked up the Rosy Room. It is a really big key and I am wearing it around my neck on GG's West Coast Eagles member lanyard. Not that Linden will be interested in vintage or history and family stuff — but I can't risk it. He will be interested if I show interest. I am thinking about taking my own bedroom key as well — thanks to his 'bush cockroach in Lily's bed' prank I have skin sensitivity issues. That night still haunts me to this day. Actually, I had to go and speak to a special therapist about it. Embarrassing! Now I do not like being tickled. FULL STOP!

Linden is still Linden. I will not waste the lead in my new pacer on writing about him.

We had our dinner, which was a delicious gnocchi with burnt butter and sage number, which GG is legendary for. Linden had plain pasta because he is a fussy eater. The phone rang and GG answered it and, while he was on the phone, Linden took a second lemonade can out of the fridge AND put one in his bedroom for later. PIG. Then he finished off the remaining chocolate ganache cake and burped into my face, the most disgusting smell.

I must say as I write this I feel alive with RAGE. I am fairly seething with rage.

Then GG came back to the dinner table and said he had to go out. And I'm like, *GG you said you would talk to Pig Boy about his behaviour and now you are leaving me alone with the psycho at nighttime.* Obviously, I couldn't say this in front of Linden so I said it telepathically with my eyebrows and my mouth turned down. GG got the message at once and said he was so sorry to be running off on Linden's first night but a friend from bridge had had a nasty fall and needed some help. He would only be a short time. GG told us there was plenty of cake but I am afraid I could not stop myself from saying, there was not … ANYMORE. And GG frowned at Linden, and Linden was like WHATEVER.

I hate him.

I took the key to my bedroom and I locked myself in. I attempted to read *Playing Beatie Bow* but I couldn't concentrate. So I put it away and got out my laptop to read — this time *The Chamber of Secrets*. I went straight to the bit where the Weasley brothers get the Ford Anglia to fly and they rescue Harry. It is very good comfort reading and it helped me tremendously, even though there is a squiggly shatter line running through the screen that makes the words jumpy. I heard my door rattle and felt good having the key around my neck, even though it was poking into my ribcage and it smelled rusty, which is my least favourite smell.

This morning I slept in and I was so angry with myself because I was supposed to get up and execute phase one. I jumped out of bed and went to find GG at the top of the table, figging up all the toast and basically ruining it. But he was not there and so I searched the laundry slash jam-making room and he was not there. Only figs and sugar and buckets — YUK!! SPEWALICIOUS! I could also see a big bag of quinces sitting on the washing machine. Quinces actually hurt my tongue and make my mouth produce too much saliva. VOMITOUS! He was not tending to the garden or watching television. It was not a bridge day and I wondered if he had nipped out to see Nimmy. But it was too early for Nimmy as she would still be in the breakfast room eating some non-crunchy food.

Then I started to panic! I looked into Linden's room and he was snoring his ugly head off. So I had the presence of mind to execute the plan. I took the finger out of my dressing gown pocket and placed it on his pillow. Then I tiptoed out and kept looking for GG.

I found him. He was asleep on his bed but he had his glasses on and was fully dressed, holding onto the bedside dresser phone. The short curly cord was stretched out straight. He cradled the two bulky plastic parts to his chest like a teddy bear. I strongly, strongly felt that something bad had happened. So I crept forward thinking *please don't let GG be dead … please don't let GG be dead*, and he must have felt me telepathically as he woke up and smiled at me.

I told GG I strongly felt something was terribly wrong, and GG started to CRY. And I thought to myself this is almost as bad as if he was dead because GG does NOT cry. I took his hand and he said, 'My dear little Lily Pilly, something is wrong. I am afraid my bridge story was a bit of a ruse. It's Nimmy. Nimmy has gone downhill and it is not looking good for her.'

I am embarrassed to say that at first, all I could see was Nimmy speeding out of control in her wheelchair down a steep hill, while shouting WOOOO HOOOOO and that made me smile. But Grandad kept on talking and I soon realised that what he meant was, she was dying. Then I started to howl and GG held me tight and he howled too but then there was a CATASTROPHIC NOISE and Linden started screaming his lungs out and came running into GG's room, screaming the words, 'BODY PART! There is a random finger on my pillow, a finger on my pillow, come and see it, come and see it … Get it off my pillow, GG!'

GG said, 'Maybe it is a worm or slug, or something of that nature — it can't possibly be a finger as all our fingers are present and accounted for,' and he was the old GG again.

I felt slightly sorry for Linden because I was, at least, sort of prepared for mystery from the Rosy

Room but to wake up with a juicy digit on your pillow slip must have come as a bit of a shock. Ba Ha Ha Linden!! Suffer in your jocks!

Grandad said, 'Please calm down, Linden, and let me change my glasses,' so he started looking around for his other pair and he couldn't find them. I slipped very quietly into Linden's room and popped Lily's finger back into my dressing gown pocket.

Linden was still screaming, 'I DID SO SEE A FINGER,' and he was all jumpy and sweaty and I have to say, even though I was drowning in sorrow for poor Nimmy I was extremely pleased that Linden was MIND-FREAKED this badly.

I heard the mirror rattle loudly like OL was doing a victory dance and then I felt terrible for her as Nimmy, her dear one, was going downhill — her absolute dearest one. And it is totally up to me to break the bad news.

I am worried this might make her flat twenty-four seven. As in ALL THE TIME.

So GG found his glasses and pulled himself together and went to see this alleged finger, which was, of course, not there. He was quite sharp with Linden but not sharp enough for my liking until Linden turned and said, 'It's Lily, Lily did it, where is the finger, turdburger?' and I started howling in *indignation* (fab new OL word) and GG really snapped BIG-TIME and shouted, 'PISH POSH! DON'T BE RIDICULOUS, LINDEN, Lily can't even stomach the look of a fig, let alone touch a detached finger. YOU IMAGINED IT.'

This is true. My disgust of figs is well known.

Then GG said Nimmy was not well and he wanted to freshen up and go back and see her. But first he had an important phone call to make. I knew he had to call his son, my dad, to tell him the bad news too.

It is later on in the day. I have not seen Nimmy or Other Lily.

So GG was on the phone and Linden made some figgy toast for himself and then ate it in his room with his earplugs in like the surly little pudding head that he is. I pulled out the key and opened the door to the Rosy Room … and the dust cloth was jiggling and jiving all over the place. OL was super excited and I wanted to say 'calm your farm or we will get busted' but I didn't have the heart. I let her have a nanosecond of joy before my bad news. The news could have thrown her into the depths of anguish for all eternity. Heavy!

So I took my time pulling off the sheet to reveal her beautiful eyes glistening with happiness and she was doing that chuckle thing which is no longer annoying but simply *delightful*. (FAVE NEW OL WORD OF ALL TIME!)

'How did it go?' she whisper-shouted joyously — and as I write this I am struck by how much fun a really good prop can be and I almost, almost understand Linden's rubber-vomit stage.

'It went very well,' I replied with as much joy as I could muster but she could tell it didn't match her joy at all as she is incredibly good at reading things like people's faces and voices. It's probably because she has been stuck in a mirror since 1947.

'What's the matter, dear one?' she asked very gently but firmly. 'Has Linden been mean to you?'

And I said, 'No, we totally nailed freaking Linden out. It's Nimmy … Lucy … she is going downhill … I just heard GG slash Colin say on the phone that she only has a few days left,' and then to make it perfectly clear, I added, 'left alive.' Then I blubbed like a baby again but Lily did not.

She leaned forward and said, 'Can I ask you a favour, dearest?'

I said, 'Yes, anything, anything at all!' but I was actually thinking, what can I do for a girl inside a mirror?

'I must see my dear one, one more time. Please, do you think you could organise it?'

And I'm like, yeah sure, I will just put the mirror in my Hello Kitty organiser and off we go. Of course I didn't say that. I did say, 'I can't promise anything but I will die trying,' and this seemed to give her confidence in me.

Then I heard Linden *rabbiting around* (GG-ism) in the kitchen for chips and biscuits so I said I must go. As I placed the sheet over the mirror, OL started to cry and she almost touched the glass.

'Stop!' I shouted — and she did. Big silent tears plopped down her face and I was completely gutted.

Eleven

So we are now going to see Nimmy. Linden did not want to come so GG said he could stay at home and watch ABC3. Linden laughed and said that is for babies but he sat down and watched it and laughed his head off at Kayne and Ambo. They are really funny — Kayne is cute but not as cute as Scotty Tweedie. The key to the Rosy Room is still around my neck and I feel glad but itchy and stinky.

I am scared to see Nimmy as I have not seen anyone dying before and it might be a bit frightening. I hope there are not too many cords and machines and stuff.

It is a very beautiful day and the weather is all springtime even though it's the middle of winter. We were in a hurry to Nimmy's this morning so we walked straight past Ms HB's house. Sometimes, we cross the road and take a bit of a detour (for our health, says GG, but I think it is because he can't stand her dogs going ballistic at the gate).

Today Ms HB was sitting outside on the padded seat in her walking frame enjoying the weather as well. I think she spends more time using the seat bit than the walking bit. She was wearing a dress that was too short and there was a gap between her hemline and her knee-length stockings and I could see her knees, which were as white as a ghost's, they contrasted much with her very tanned pantyhose. She shouted out, 'Yoo-hoo, Colin and little Lindy, how are we today? Terrific weather we are having, isn't it? Care for a cordial?'

And GG actually said, 'That plurry woman!' (*plurry* is an almost-swearword old people use when they get cross) under his breath just so I could hear, and then he said breezily, 'So sorry, Ms HB, we are in a bit of a hurry. Lucy is not too well at the moment.'

Ms HB replied, 'Sorry to hear that. Now … dear Colin, I won't ask you again, please dear … do call me Dawn.' Then she tried to straighten up to show off her big bosoms. At first I was shocked — Ms HB was getting her flirt on with my GRANDFATHER — but then I had a light-bulb moment. It was as bright as GG's fluorescent hallway light that has a broken shade. MS HB IS DAWN HORNBUCKLE … THE HORRIBLE GIRL FROM DOWN THE STREET … AND SHE WAS HITTING ON GG! — except she was most certainly not a girl anymore. She was totally ancient.

I was in a state of shock. I felt more upset than when I found the finger. That was a mystery. This is plain VOMITOUS.

GG did not seem surprised and said in his charming voice, 'We must be getting along,' and then held my hand tightly and although we walked away at a normal pace, GG's face was saying he wanted to run.

I am back home now at GG's even though Nimmy is not dead … yet.

In the end, it really wasn't that scary. At first, it was flat-out off-putting — Nimmy was lying in her bed and her eyes were closed but her face said that she was in Nimmy Land twenty-four seven. I tried to imagine Nimmy Land full of babies, shoes, boxes, swing music, cakes and a Colin with hair … and of course her dearest sister. This helped me tremendously and I was even able to take her hand and stroke its gnarly old skin. (Note to self: sunscreen is very important genetically for me.)

GG sat on the other side and held her other hand, the one with all the twisty jewellery. He said lovely things to her about John and Letty and all of us … and about Paris in 1957 and Cairo in 1962 etc etc etc. And then he went on about the rose garden … and he even managed to say something nice about Linden. He said he was a strong, good-looking fellow with a healthy appetite and left it at that, which was very kind of him.

Apparently I am a sheer delight.

Then Nimmy sat up and opened her eyes and said, 'Home,' and as she said it, a whole lot of brown stuff came out of her mouth and I screamed and GG hit the emergency button and nurses came running.

The brown stuff was tea and then we saw the tea sippy cup next to her. The matron apologised and said she'd forgotten to phone and tell us that Nimmy became conscious again this morning and had asked for tea and her dear one. She particularly wanted her sister, whom they had never seen visit, so they hoped she might settle for tea. And she did, she took a sip and fell straight back to sleep. Only problem was she forgot to swallow it.

Then the matron looked at me and asked, 'Were you named after anyone special in the family?' I shrugged because I didn't want to alert GG I am onto the secret, even if he is not. And the truth is, I am not sure if I am named after her or if it was one of those *Freudian coincidences* Fern keeps banging on about, like somewhere in the deep grooves of Dad's brain he remembers a pretty girl in a mirror named Lily.

The matron smiled at me, which is odd because usually she is like super busy swishing around. She only stops to spray her hair with more hairspray behind the nurses' station and then she is off again being bossy but friendly. Then she asked, 'Who is Edgar?'

I shrugged in a noncommittal way. I'm getting really good at shrugging.

GG was a bit flustered but stayed strong for Nimmy and me.

After a while, the matron and the other nurses left and GG settled down. Sophie, our special nice nurse, stayed on. She asked GG if Lucy really did have a sister because last night she had been calling for her. It was two-thirty in the morning and the matron decided not to phone as Lucy's vital signs were good for a dying person. Then Sophie lowered her voice and added that Lucy had managed to limp into her ensuite and there Sophie had found her banging on the bathroom mirror … calling out for Lily, her dear, dear sister, her dearest one. There was a bit of mumbling about her mama and pa too. At first, they thought she was calling for me and having the usual delusions and mixing everything up but something — the nurses and matron were not sure what that something was — made them feel like Nimmy was really remembering when she pleaded, '*Please Edgar, please let her go, please I beg you.*' The matron was stunned and a bit unnerved as she had given Nimmy extra medicine, which usually makes her drowsy. It takes all the pain away and sends her on the express train to Nimmy Land ... but not this time. Apparently, Nimmy lay her forehead on the glass and whispered, 'I am sorry, dear Lily.' Sophie said that it took three nurses and the matron to get her back into bed.

And I did stop myself from saying, 'YES, SHE HAS A NON-IDENTICAL TWIN SISTER WHO HAS BEEN STUCK IN THE MIRROR SINCE NINETEEN FORTY-SEVEN!' Instead, I looked at GG and thought to myself, *Well, go on, Colin ... who is this sister that is never spoken of. Not even once.*

And GG looked at me and said Lucy did have a twin sister named Lily who mysteriously disappeared in the summer of 1947. It was in all the newspapers.

She vanished without a trace. The Dunnings were incredibly brave and carried on very well but Lucy never ever EVER wanted to discuss it. She ended up inheriting the house and he was very happy to live there, as it is a wonderfully big house with terrific bones. But Lucy tended to spend a lot of time in Lily's old bedroom and he let her because it seemed to rally her spirits no end. Then he said Lucy was very secretive about the room and the disappearance and so it just naturally happened that her sister was never mentioned and forgotten. GG lowered his voice and said one of the main reasons dear Lucy had to go into the Home was because night after night she would get up and bang on the mirror. One night she got so agitated, she threw her favourite Bohemian cut crystal vase at the mirror and the vase smashed into smithereens. She was screaming, 'Lily!' Poor GG continued on bravely and said that was when he realised he couldn't manage anymore. He was frightened Lucy might hurt herself. He dabbed at his eyes with his tissue.

And I am so so glad that I know Lily.

She is NOT NOT NOT NOT forgotten, not ever.

When Sophie left, GG said he wanted to go and find a cup of tea as he was feeling a titch headachy. When he left, I whispered into Nimmy's ear, 'Lily is going very well and she misses you heaps too.' I hoped that Nimmy's eyelids might flicker in recognition but they didn't.

Grandad made some more phone calls in the corridor and I heard things like 'strong heart', 'feisty spirit' and 'my dear one' in his cracking voice.

Then it was time to go because the rest of my family will be arriving soon to say goodbye to Nimmy. Mum and Dad are flying in from their anniversary holiday. Zinnia is arriving shortly from Spain with Manuel. Fern is already driving down from Perth with the three munted Angora cats. And of course, Linden is sitting on the couch waiting too. There is only one turdburger in this family and that is Linden. He only has to walk three streets, not catch two planes and a bus.

TURDBURGER EXTREME.

But as we were leaving to go get supplies for three

random cats (because no doubt Fern would have forgotten to pack their food) and food for the eight of us, the very nice nurse Sophie caught up with us in the car park. I thought Nimmy must be dead because she looked kind of agitated and shy.

Sophie said she was going on holidays with her friend — they were meant to go on a bushwalk but the friend had just texted and said she had twisted her ankle. She showed us the photo the friend sent and the ankle was enormous and disgusting so they wouldn't be walking anywhere for a few days … but Sophie still had leave, starting from this afternoon at two pm, and because there were so many of us and because she was so fond of Nimmy and because Nimmy has asked her every day for four years could she go home, she said she would be honoured to nurse Nimmy in GG's house and, 'Would he consider taking his Miss Lucy home?'

Well, GG looked so pleased and even though his mouth was smiling, it wobbled all over his chin. I was so happy I shouted 'Yay' out loud, which was way babyish but I couldn't even be bothered being embarrassed. I actually gave Sophie a hug AND a high five and she looked incredibly pleased. The IMPOSSIBLE might be happening.

Sophie and GG went back into the Home as they had to check with the matron and get permission and stuff because apparently it is going to be *a logistical nightmare*.

Twelve

I was happy to walk home by myself because I knew Fern was nearly at GG's house and suddenly I wanted to see my own sister. Even though I do not like her I do love her, plus I wanted to see what Linden did to the cats.

As I turned into our street I remembered about Dawn. The memory of the bright pink scar on Lily's ankle rushed into my brain and I started to feel seriously angry. I could even hear my heart pumping blood through my ears and each thump was telling me to punch Dawn in the head even though she was an old lady. I have never felt like this — even with Linden.

I walked past really slowly and there she was.

'Hello Lindy,' Dawn shouted out all sickly sweet.

And then it was like I was channelling Harry Potter because I felt brave enough to say, 'It's Lily, I was named after my great-aunty Lily. L-I-L-Y DUNNINGS.' Although that statement might be an erroneous lie, it rolled right off my tongue really nicely so maybe it's true after all.

Dawn's purple eyelids went all squinty as she looked at me over her triple chins. This made me feel even crosser and so I asked, 'How is dear Chompers these days?'

'Chompers? What are you talking about, girl?' And you could actually see her brain trying to remember the poor dog ... tick ... tock ... tick ... tock ... until eventually ... it did remember. Then Dawn said, 'Chompers has been dead since 1952, he is buried over there by the gate under the Vinca plants. How did you know I once had a dog named Chompers?' She grabbed her Zimmer frame and bolted over to the gate where I was standing. Meanwhile, her two very much alive but really skinny dogs were going psycho and I began to feel scared, but only of pain and not of Dawn and the dogs.

And then I amazed myself as I got all mystical and mysterious and whispered, 'Lily speaks to me from the Otherside,' and just so Dawn got my vibe, I pointed to the sky.

Dawn's goggly eyes followed my finger and she looked up. Now it was her turn to feel scared even though she pretended not to be. She laughed and said, 'Oh yes? And what does that little blonde brat have to say?' like she was humouring me.

I answered, 'She says you are a big bully and that she is WATCHING YOU all the time. She showed me her ankle, not very nice of you, Dawn, not very nice at all.'

And Dawn's bottom lip began to wobble as she whispered, 'How do you know about the ankle?'

I pointed up to the sky again and looked happy like Other Lily was waving at me from a nearby cloud. And so I went on, 'Who could forget the 12th of December 1947 when an enormous tortured dog chases you down the street, rips you off your Malvern

Star and tries to eat your ankle!'

I know it was just a spooky coincidence but the two dogs went very quiet. The timing was freaky but probably they were exhausted because they are so thin. So I kept on talking. 'How you treated Chompers and all your dogs is disgusting. Disgusting!' and then I did get a bit carried away and I finished up with, 'You haven't got long to live, Dawn Hornbuckle, so you'd better make amends!' Mum is forever telling us to make amends because life is short and precious.

Then I walked off quick smart, and Dawn shuffled closer to the gate and leant over it shouting out very dramatically that she was very sorry and, 'Please Lily, please forgive me.' I turned around to find her looking up at the sky. She looked really pathetic and I felt a bit sorry for her and so I quickly added, 'Lily says she forgives you,' and watched as a lovely smile spread across Dawn's face. She didn't look so ugly. She looked kind of nice, but then I remembered the other thing and I shouted, 'Lily says to STAY AWAY FROM LUCY'S COLIN, NOW AND FOREVER!'

Dawn said, 'Yes I will, consider it done!'

I kept walking, feeling shaky and sick but over the moon with joy.

When I got home and opened the front door, I found the good room in a big mess. There were chips and cushions and a spilt half-empty mug of Milo and magazines and newspapers everywhere.

I totally flipped out, I shouted, 'What happened here because it looks like a wild boar on a rampage has gone through GG's good room.'

Linden said, 'Nothing happened … I got bored and hungry.'

So I said, 'Nimmy is dying and Fern and EVERYONE is coming here soon to say goodbye.' My voice cracked unintentionally but very dramatically.

He replied, 'She is old. CARE FACTOR — ZERO!'

And I am utterly speechless and beyond cross.

Without thinking, I found myself going into my bedroom to find the hidden finger. I tucked it into my pocket and went back into the good room and plopped it right into Linden's Milo while he was laughing his head off at some stupid children's cartoon. Linden always, always finishes off his Milo with an enormous slurp and then he sticks his own finger into his cup and scrapes off all the sugar and crunchy bits. Vomitous behaviour. Shake hands with Original Lily, Pig Boy!

And so I started cleaning up with great indignation until I remembered the good news that Nimmy might be coming home and that Dawn was going to start behaving herself. By this stage, Linden had rammed his earplugs back in and was starting to gyrate on the sofa like a frying piece of bacon crackling in GG's extra large pan. WEIRD MUCH?

So I took out the key and visited OL. She was waiting for me and almost touching the glass with anticipation. I said straight off that everything is okay and that Nimmy was not dead yet and she might, just might be coming home thanks to a very nice nurse called Sophie and a twisted ankle friend.

Lily was completely silent with joy and started rocking back and forth like she was trying to keep the joy in. Kind of unnerving! I had to get my nerves together and tell her that Nimmy coming home was only a might, a probably, and not a guaranteed thing. I was worried that she would explode into tiny parallel universe pieces if she didn't see her Lucy dearest soon.

This freaked me out and so I quickly changed the subject and said that Linden was pure evil and that I hope she didn't mind but I'd gone straight to phase two and dropped her finger into his Milo. OL looked at her hand in a curious way and replied she didn't mind at all and hoped he had a nasty choke on it.

She went quiet for a minute then finally said, 'Years ago, before it was lost — and only sometimes and not always — I could make the finger wiggle and wave. If Lucy held it up for me and I concentrated hard, it would move. It would give us both such a blast that Lucy would roll around on the ground dying with laughter.'

OL and I both went very quiet and I guess it was because Lucy is dying for real this time.

When I was done feeling *maudlin* (I feel this word is totally me), I went to ask OL would she like me to read to her or something, while we waited for the pig to make his big discovery. I even picked up her favourite copy of *Biggles* but as I turned the pages I could feel a very sorrowful silence coming from the mirror. It was not in the least bit maudlin but it was very intense. My vibe detector was totally shrieking ALERT! BIG-TIME. So I looked up from *Biggles* (who was getting into his plane … again … beyond boring … I don't understand why she likes it so much!) to find that OL was looking past me and at the old dusty furniture. Her blue eyes were wide and watery and I could see her hands trembling like she was being gripped by something terrible.

'Lily!' I shouted, 'What is the matter … apart from the obvious?' (Dying sister and long-term entrapment etc etc.)

OL was quiet for a long time and I knew she was thinking of how to say something that is upsetting in a non-upsetting way, but then it all just spurted out anyway.

'I am being as dull as dishwater. I do apologise. It's just that lately I really do feel weak, I feel like a paper cut-out dolly that needs to be glued to stiff cardboard to keep me upright.'

BINGO. OL totally nailed her new condition.

I was torn. Did I mention to her that in the last couple of days, she disappeared whenever she turned sideways? The whole dying sister thing was enough at the mo. A tiny bit of logic in my brain told me that perhaps these two things were connected.

But OL rallied and repeated the words, 'Chin up, chin up, chin up,' which I think means be brave and positive. She brightened and said, 'Wouldn't it be fun if I could wiggle my finger and give Linden the biggest fright in the world?'

I replied the finger was in the good room sitting in a cup on the coffee table by the bookcase and OL breathed in deeply and put her fingers on her temples and whispered, 'I am visualising the finger in the Milo cup and I am commanding it to wiggle in a most violent and obvious manner.'

She spread her hands out and wiggled each finger in turn until she came to the empty spot. She clenched her eyes shut and I could almost feel the electricity zapping off her and down into the good room. She opened one eye and said, 'Go and see if it is working because it will be a jolly good spectacle indeed.'

I lowered the dust sheet over the mirror, leaving OL looking constipated in deep concentration. I whispered, 'Goodbye, I will be back shortly.'

I tiptoed down the passage and peered between the crack in the doorway, just in time to see bubbles coming out of the top of the cup. There was a *veritable* (no idea as to meaning but feel it really suits) cappuccino froth going on but Pig Boy did not notice because he was going crazy over a new violent movie that was being advertised loudly on the telly.

Just when I thought all dear OL's energy was being wasted on this pudding head, he picked up the Milo and started to drink it — but his eyes were still glued to the screen and he didn't notice the finger slip down onto his tongue. And this is when he did start to notice it. He screamed and had conniptions beyond belief and literally vomited up the rest of the Milo in a chunky custard style. And there in the middle of GG's good room mat was Lily's pointer finger waving and wiggling like it was possessed. It was grooving and flexing like a gymnast on fast-forward. It was KERAZEE TOWN.

I opened the door and just stood there and my mouth was actually gaping open. It was like bizarro world had arrived at GG's. It was a good thing I looked so shocked because Linden pushed past me screaming as he bolted to the front door. He actually screamed, 'Mutant body part. Run for your life, Lily!' as the finger started to propel its way forward like it was spring-loaded. I watched him run out onto the street and keep on running.

HUZZAH, LOSER! OINK-I-TY OINK OINK!

Thirteen

I ran and snatched up the finger and quickly rinsed and dried it and then I burst into the Rosy Room, ripped off the dust sheet and held up the finger like it was made of gold!!

'TA DA!' I said, 'Best dancing finger in the world!' Even if it's highly plausible it is the *only* dancing finger in the world.

'Did I wriggle it? Did it move?' she asked anxiously.

And I answered, 'It totally rock-and-rolled, Lily!'

'What is this rock-and-roll again?' Sometimes I forget she has been in the mirror for sixty-something years.

'Never mind, what I mean is, it worked!' I stopped and tried to remember an old-fashioned dance and then I said, 'It foxtrotted, shimmied and strutted like crazy.'

And OL was delighted with this news. Then she said, 'When you popped me in the Milo I got a warm sensation up my hand, which has never happened before.'

But then she slumped to the ground and said, 'Dear me, I am quite exhausted from the exertion!' Nanna Pinkie is prone to saying this and then she has a nanna nap and feels better. I began to feel very worried for OL. Something was changing about her. It seems the weaker Nimmy gets the more out of shape Other Lily becomes. And that's a seriously sad thought. Though I have only met OL a few days ago, I feel like I have known her all my life. We are kindred beyond words.

But then I remembered Deadly Dawn! Double Whammy!!

And so I said, 'I bumped into your good friend Dawn.' (sarcasm MUCH?)

'Oh, I knew she never moved house but I thought (read — hoped) she might have snuffed it,' OL said.

'She is lumpy and old and on her way out, but she has all her marbles (Dad-ism for *not crazy*) and she is after Colin!'

OL shouted, 'Not still!'

'Still? What is this *still* business?' I said.

'Lucy told me that Dawn would flirt with Colin in the most open and obvious manner. One time at a mutual friend's wedding, Dawn drank three shandies and put her hand on Colin's knee! Lucy was beyond livid. Outrageous and disgusting behaviour.'

I now didn't feel so bad about getting a bit OTT with my 'make amends' finale. So I told OL exactly what happened and what I said to dear old Dawn (not).

OL was delighted I'd given Dawn a fright but beyond outraged that Dawn's new old dogs are still skinny and mean. So I promised I'd check on them before I leave GG's house and if they did not look happier and healthier I was going to call the RSPCA. Then we were both really sad because I don't want to leave her ever and OL doesn't want me to go.

I pulled out one of the drawers of the mirror's wooden base to hide the finger in a safe spot. Inside it was a small pile of yellowing crinkly newspapers dated from 23 December 1947. These old papers had articles on Other Lily and her mysterious disappearance. I read the first article. There was a photo underneath it. It is the photo of OL and Lucy holding onto a cat, except the photo had been cropped and enlarged and so it's just of OL's face. She is soooo pretty. I cut out the first newspaper article and have stuck it in my journal. There are heaps of them — mostly they are about how OL's disappearance is still a mystery.

MYSTERIOUS DISAPPEARANCE OF LOCAL GIRL

Dec. 23.

Christmas preparations in the small south west town of Treebark have ceased as the town searches for one of its brightest and most promising young students, thirteen-year-old Miss Lily Beryl Dunnings of Flotsam Road.

Her twin sister, Miss Lucy Dunnings, last saw the missing girl out the front of the family's Edwardian home. She confirmed

Lily was practising cartwheels and handstands and then stopped to make a daisy chain. This has been verified by neighbours from across the road, a Mr and Mrs F. Daglish.

Miss Lucy Dunnings says that was the last time she saw her sister outside of the house.

Mr Kenneth Dunnings (of Dunnings Hardware and Nursery) and his wife, Mrs Beryl Dunnings (CWA best sponge cake winner, 1936 to present), declined to comment as they are overcome with worry.

The alarm was raised by Miss Janet Knoblett, a recent graduate teacher to Lily and Lucy. Miss Knoblett visited the Dunnings on the 22nd with a tin of chocolates for the family as they had shown great kindness to her in her first teaching post far from her home. She found the family 'in a state of absolute chaos' as they searched for Lily. Miss Knoblett was asked to notify Sergeant Glendennings, who authorised a search party. The Dunnings family could not shed any further light on the disappearance.

I put the papers aside, wrapped up the finger and placed it in one of the smaller boxes by itself. And that's when I had another idea.

'Lily?' I asked with trepidation because I did not want to get her hopes up, 'Can you feel your finger? Even in the slightest bit?'

And she answered, 'Why no, dear heart, that is why it was lost for many a year and I am so grateful to you for finding it.'

But I continued on, 'You said you felt a warm sensation in your hand before?'

'I certainly can't feel the finger jiggle, but I must admit,' and then she hesitated, 'I must admit that just after the warmth, I felt a cold tingle.'

'Like running water?'

'Yes!' she squeaked.

And so this is my idea.

In Harry Potter, portals are opening and closing all the time and perhaps, just perhaps — this is not a guaranteed fact but an idea I am having — this mirror portal might be opening up now for the first time since Edgar the Pudding Head cast his terrible spell. And it's somehow related to Nimmy dying. And this is why Lily has some sensation in her finger.

To test my theory I asked OL if she had any sensation where her tippy-toe might be.

'No, nothing of the sort.'

'Try to look a little deeper,' I urged her.

So she closed her eyes and then lifted her missing toe leg up and pointed it at me, then all of a sudden her foot swivelled in the direction of the pile in the corner. So I went to the corner and there were chocolate tins and shoeboxes and patterns for awesome cotton frocks and, underneath the delightful junk, was a pretty red sewing basket. Apparently it belonged to Beryl who said it was strictly 'out of bounds', as it contained her sharpest Art Nouveau sterling silver sewing scissors WITH Floral Repousse handles from the Motherland and 'could not be replaced for love or money.'

'It's in the sewing basket,' gasped OL, as if she was a magician or something and I, her faithful assistant, opened the basket and started to take out measuring tapes and loads of cotton bobbins and the hallowed scissors and scraps of what is now vintage material but at the time it was cutting-edge fashion. There were so many cool sewing patterns that I got a bit distracted. (Note to self: learn how to sew awesome vintage stuff.)

When I came across the special scissors, they were wrapped in velvet, like the Queen's best brooch. I unwrapped them to reveal the freakiest scissors in the entire world. They actually had horrible little flowers all over the handles AND at the bottom of the blades were two little kids' faces popping out of roses. The children's eyes were rolled in toward each other like they were asking the other one, 'What's up?' It was plain creepy … more like 'What's up with Beryl?'

I got worried the toe was not in the sewing basket because I couldn't see it. I lifted everything carefully because even though I am now used to the finger, a large piece of toe with a scratchy broken nail was a bit of a spew-making thought.

'I can't see it,' I told OL, and she closed her eyes and started to really get into the vibe of it.

‘It is definitely in there,’ she said, ‘keep looking.’

Just then, I spied a little blue box of pins and my vibe was very strong that the tippy-toe was inside it. And I was right. I opened it up and there, sitting on a nest of pins, was the toe, still plump and fresh. There was a bit of dirt under the nail but nothing too much.

I held it up like a trophy and OL clapped her hands in sheer delight. I moved toward the mirror so she could have a good look at it and after a minute or two she gazed at me with her big blue eyes and said, ‘What do you think this means?’

My mind was swirling with possibilities and all seven of the Potter books hit me hard in the head — one at a time. Kerplunk! Kerplunk! Kerpow! Not literally, of course, but I now know that anything is possible.

I answered that this is a very promising turn of events and promise is a very good thing indeed. And I really, really, really wanted to touch the glass … and I nearly did as fingerprints are overrated but pain is not.

I shook my head because even in my own head I dare not think what it might mean. That either the best thing in the world might be happening — that Other Lily comes out of the mirror. Or that it's the worst thing in the world — that she is dying too. Why is she becoming like a faded postcard? Alarming! If she can now feel stuff, maybe she can age too. Maybe she is reconnecting with our time and could shrivel up in the mirror and turn into one of those old skinny ladies that wander around at the Home smiling at everyone with lopsided lipstick. (Except without the lipstick … obviously.)

Other Lily has been in the mirror for sixty-seven years. When she went into the mirror, Queen Elizabeth was all young and pretty plus she was getting married to a handsome prince who was adorable but now looks like a naughty goblin. The Queen is still very pretty for a very old lady. There are some old newspaper clippings in a shoebox of the bride and groom looking happy. In today's newspaper, the couple is on page seven … still smiling and looking happyish.

Maybe OL will turn into an eighty-year-old just like that and the shock of rapidly aging organs will explode and kill her. Then she will be a puddle in the mirror. I can't feel a vibe on this one. Something is changing, OL can feel stuff but she is now as flat as one of Zinnia's old DVDs all the time. I am very worried but still very excited. It is a paradoxical thing.

Just then I heard a knock on the front door so I quickly put the toe with the finger in the drawer and said a quick goodbye to OL. I locked the Rosy Room and ran to answer the front door. It was Fern, of course, and she had the three peeved cats in a cat travelling box, wailing like they really had been cleaved open with an axe.

Fern hugged me tightly and said, 'How are you, Lily Pilly?' and I replied with great indignation, 'I am fine, Frondsy.' This made her laugh (odd girl) and then she waved her arms around dramatically and slapped her hand to her head and exclaimed, 'I have forgotten the cat food,' and I replied, 'It is alright because GG has remembered it and will pick some up on the way home from the Home.'

'Bless,' sighed Fern like GG is a leprechaun or a gnome, but he is neither.

Then there was another knock on the door and it was the man from Silver Chain. He had all kinds of stuff to make Nimmy comfortable for her last few days. He went about measuring and setting up stuff in GG and Nimmy's bedroom and made lists and then went away and came back with more stuff. Soon Nimmy and GG's room looked a bit like the Home, so I went and cut some roses from the ancient rosebush and put them into a vase. I thought this was a lovely touch but I am still bleeding.

So it really truly must be happening — Nimmy is coming home! Yay! But it is such a long way to the Rosy Room from this bedroom off the front door that it might as well be to Antarctica. Will it be enough for OL to have her dear one in the same house? I was starting to feel one of my highly suggestible states coming on and that I could easily slip into hysteria. So I went into the kitchen and grabbed some cake and a paper bag and breathed deeply until I felt I was able to eat the cake without being sick.

Next thing I knew, Sophie the nurse was knocking on the door and she had more stuff from the Home, but she was wearing her own clothes and looked different. She looked younger and she had put in her second ear-pierced earrings and was wearing her long blonde hair out of her usual tight bun. Quite Awesome.

Sophie said the ambulance was transporting Lucy right now because she was reasonably stable at the moment. So Nimmy and GG are in the back of the ambulance like they are riding in a horse-drawn coach — just like the Queen and her Prince in 1947.

Fourteen

It is UNBELIEVABLY DIFFICULT to get some privacy and peace around here at the mo. There is SO MUCH going on that it is impossible to sneak into the Rosy Room as much as I would like to. (I know Other Lily is going bonkers with anxiety and anticipation.) Other Lily has had an idea but she needs me to execute it. *Execute* is a bizarre word for carrying out a plan. I can't stay long with her and the more nervous I get, the more difficult it is to get the key in the door. Stress City. Other Lily is rattling like crazy and she is lucky the house is so noisy and full of people because otherwise we would be busted for sure.

My family members keep on arriving!

Yesterday

Fern — 11.05 am drove in her Hyundai with traumatised cats.

Today

Mum and Dad — 12.42 am took a plane home and then drove the Subaru down.

Zinnia and Manuel — 5.22 pm took two planes and a bus and a taxi.

Linden (AKA Pig Boy) is here already, which is a *darn* shame (old-fashioned swearword that is nicer than new-fashioned swearwords).

Linden and Fern are not talking because Fern has unfriended Linden on Facebook, thanks to a funny cat meme that offended her big-time. Zinnia and Manuel are speaking in Spanish all the time. I asked Zinnia what they were saying and she said they were angry that the taxi driver ripped them off. I thought they were declaring their passionate love for each other, it sounded so good.

Fern, Zinnia and Manuel are planning a trip across Europe with their old friends. Apparently, travelling across Europe used to be called 'touring the Continent', because good old GG piped up and said he and Nimmy had done that. So then Zinnia was desperate to get into the Rosy Room and find all the old letters and photos. PAR AVION? NO WAY JOSÉ!

GG asked me if I had found them and I said no, I knew nothing about the tart box of blue aerogrammes but I was your girl if you were looking for the perfect pavlova. GG smiled at me in a funny way. Then he tried to open the door but of course it was locked. He looked for the key, which normally hung on the wall, but it was not there. Of course it was digging into me. GG turned and looked carefully into my face and I looked back. I was hoping my vibe was travelling telepathically into his brain. And then finally GG totally got me. Sure, he had no idea of what he was 'getting', but he was on Team Lily … pending an explanation. Grandad then turned to Zinnia and said, 'Oh Zinnzy, I have misplaced the key, I will look for it later. So sorry.'

And Fern was like, 'Oh GG, don't worry about it, we can look for it later,' and Zinnia dabbed at her eyes and smiled and said, 'Yes, later GG,' like he was dying too.

And then Fern gave me a look that said, 'Hope GG isn't losing it?' and I looked into the distance and sighed as if to say, 'The poor darling,' and Zinnia smiled at me. She is so pretty when she smiles. Meanwhile, the key was all caught up in my crop top and singlet straps and had worked its way under my armpit and was sweating like crazy.

Nimmy slept through all of this. She had an open-mouth snore going on that showed the gap where her front tooth used to be and it was a bit off-putting. She was a full-time resident of Nimmy Land and I hoped she was thinking about pretty patterned material and jiggling wiggling fingers, and that she might see Beryl and Ken soon.

Everyone was getting on everyone else's nerves so Sophie took Nimmy's vital signs and told GG and everyone it was okay to go and have a walk around the park because it was only three streets away. I said I don't want to walk, I want to read my book, so they left me in the good room and I watched until they wandered higgledy-piggledy around the corner in a multi-size pack and out of sight! Hurrah!

Mum and Dad were sleeping because they are so old and jetlagged. Sophie was having a nap in the easy recliner chair in GG and Nimmy's room. She was out cold, poor thing — her shift at the Home had started at 4.30 this morning. I knew I must be quiet or the plan would be ruined.

I took the finger out of my pocket and very gently stroked Nimmy's scaly old face with it. Then I opened up her hand, placed the finger in it and closed the hand up. Nimmy did not stir at all and I got scared I was too late. I watched her closely and I also watched Sophie closely and she was still napping away.

Five minutes later, Nimmy woke up and tried to say something but the words were all mixed up and back to front. Sophie was still snoring her box off. PHEW!

This is when things started to happen.

Nimmy opened her hand and saw the finger and looked hard at it. Then her eyes looked to me and they opened just a little bit wider, like she was trying to say, 'Am I really holding Lily dearest's finger again?' and I answered with words and said, 'Yes, it is really Lily,' and then Nimmy's papery old gnarled hand squeezed hard and opened, and the finger danced for her. It was waltzing on the palm of her hand. Nimmy's eyes looked to me as if to say, 'You are seeing this too, I am not crazy?' And I answered with words, 'You are not crazy. It is Lily doing her thing … especially for you.'

Out of the corner of my eye I caught a strange metal thing with wheels sitting under the window, and as I looked harder at it I realised it was Nimmy's wheelchair and then I had an idea. It was an awesomely scary idea that could have gone very wrong. But once I had the idea, there was no way I could forget it and I had to move quickly.

Nimmy's eyes were closed and she had a lovely smile on her face as I raced over to the wheelchair to set it up. It took two attempts and I got my finger caught and I could not stop myself from shouting out, 'OUCH.' This woke up Sophie and she caught me with the wheelchair by Nimmy's bed, with my hand under my arm and tears running down my face. She said, 'Lily sweetheart, what is going on?'

I had the presence of mind to say I was going to take Nimmy for a stroll around the garden as the weather was delightful and GG said she really loved her garden.

Then I had to sit through a bit of a lecture on why this was not a good idea and this was when I slipped into a highly suggestible state to the POINT OF NO RETURN as I blubbed, 'Listen, Sophie, I am not an idiot but you have to believe me that Nimmy needs to go to the Rosy Room right now, while she is stable, even if I am not.' And then it was like Nimmy heard me and was completely on Team Lily-times-two because she opened her hand and out rolled the dancing finger and I shouted, 'Go for it, Lily,' and she did. And Sophie did not run away screaming like Pig Boy, she actually sat down on the bed and looked at the twirling finger very carefully and calmly, although her mouth was wide open and I could actually see her molar fillings on the left side. She was so cool and composed and then I remembered she was a trained professional.

Then she said something that no adult has ever said to me. She asked, 'What would you like me to do?'

So it was time for my mouth to flop open as I shouted, 'WHEELCHAIR … NOW … COAST CLEAR.' I couldn't get proper sentences out and my mind was whizzing along like a wheelchair on a forty-five degree angle.

With two gentle moves, Sophie got Nimmy into the chair and Nimmy's eyes opened wide like we had supercharged her or something. This was scary but good. She was awake but I had no idea if she was in Nimmy Land or Lily Land at this stage. I threw her lap rug over her and opened the door. I whispered to Sophie, 'It's safe to proceed,' as I really wanted to be all professional too. I got my Hermione Granger groove on as there was no room for erroneous mistakes.

I could tell Other Lily was seriously conniptive because the mirror was rattling like crazy and I was totally channelling Hermione because as we whizzed past Dad and Mum's bedroom I had the presence of mind to say, 'Darn those buses and trucks,' like GG does when the house rattles a lot.

Sadly, I went back to being plain old Lily as I fumbled for the key (I know I am throwing an allergic reaction, I can feel the eczema growing!) and I had a lot of trouble getting the wretched thing into the old misshapen lock. Sophie took the key from me and unlocked the door.

Nimmy was sitting up like the Queen in her carriage. Her eyes were like pretty blue stars and my brain screamed silently, *Nimmy please leave your special place just for a mo!*

I was getting frightened Other Lily was going to shatter the mirror; she was absolutely going off like a frog in a sock. Her hands were clasped together and she was rocking backward and forward like a skittle about to topple over.

I ran into the room and they followed. As Sophie

took her eyes off Nimmy for the first time she looked up and saw Other Lily being joyous beyond belief on the wrong side of the mirror. Her mouth dropped open again and this time I could see her fillings on the right side. There were not as many.

I whispered, 'This is Other Lily, well, THE Lily actually … she did disappear in 1947 but only to a parallel universe in the mirror.'

Sophie tried to speak but found she couldn't and even though we have discussed Harry Potter in depth, I got the feeling she really thought that magic was just in stories and books. She put the brakes on for Nimmy and sat down on the ground, in a way that could be described as falling over.

Other Lily waved politely with the missing finger hand but she couldn't take her eyes off her dear one. Sophie and I couldn't take our eyes off the pair of them. OL was fit to burst with happiness but Nimmy was partying on in Nimmy Land which, I have to say, annoyed me at this point in time. Meanwhile, OL was getting so excited that she ALMOST touched the glass and I ALMOST had to shout at her, 'GET BACK

FROM THE GLASS UNLESS YOU WANT TO LOSE THE END OF YOUR NOSE FOR HEAVEN'S SAKE.'

I whispered loudly in Nimmy's ear that her dear one, Lily, was here with her once again and slowly, very slowly, Nimmy's eyes came into some sort of focus and she lifted her hand slowly and leaned toward the mirror and whispered, 'Lily dearest,' with little dew drops of tears falling down her face.

Other Lily answered, 'Yes, it's me, we are in the Rosy Room together again.'

And I have to stop writing now as I am crying and smudging the pacer.

Other Lily moved so close to the mirror that I could see the pretty weave in her cotton dress. I could see that her buttons were green and her skin was tanned. I could see that she was crying with happiness and … whoops there I go again.

Okay I am back. I needed tissues and cake. There was only fig loaf left in the tin but after my recent experiences I feel mature enough now to enjoy it with a lot of butter.

What happened next can only be described as a feat of strength and pure love. And MAGIC of course. Nimmy stood up and held out both hands, leaned into the mirror and grabbed her sister's hands and SHE PULLED HER OUT OF THE MIRROR.

Total headspin.

Suddenly, there was Other Lily in real life and she hugged Nimmy and kissed her old wrinkly cheek and Nimmy very gently put her hand on Other Lily's face and said, 'Goodbye dearest.' She started breathing heavily … a kind of shallow pant … but managed to turn to Sophie and me with her eyes and they said, *Thank you, dear girls.* She looked over my shoulder and I wondered if she was seeing Beryl and Ken in homemade angelic costumes, so I turned around and there were GG and Linden. In my hysteria, I had forgotten to shut the door.

Grandad was crying and Linden was very quiet

and had a look on his face that could have passed for a human with feelings.

Nimmy whispered, 'Goodbye Col,' with a smile so beautiful that I didn't even notice the missing tooth. I don't think GG ever did notice it.

But Nimmy was beyond tired and OL held her tightly while she slumped back into her chair. Her Colin moved forward and placed his cheek on her head. Nimmy was still holding OL's hand … but her eyes were closing

We knew Lucy Griffin was moving on from the Rosy Room.

Fifteen

Apparently GG and Linden came home early as they had broken off from the rest of the group to have a little chat about 'the benefits of an improved attitude' and that's how they got to witness the very good magic. So I guess if Linden was a woody wise tree instead of an oinker, GG may have not got to say goodbye.

GG is old and can only deal with one thing at a time so he was totally focused on loving Nimmy. So only Sophie, Linden and I watched as something of an extraordinary nature was happening to OL during all of this. For the first few seconds, she was dewy and lifelike with real freckly tanned flesh and real bouncy golden curls. But when Nimmy died, she began to flatten and pixilate like GG's television screen during a bad storm.

Other Lily smiled forlornly as her whole body jittered. The wobble became a fuzzy whirl and suddenly she slipped from standing near the wheelchair and INTO a chocolate tin on the ground. I could see her pretty blue eyes looking up wistfully at me.

I picked up the tin and clutched her to my tummy even though the bottom of the tin was so tarnished and old it had crumbly rust coming off it and onto my hands and shirt.

This had exceeded my wildest imagination. My brain hurt. Other Lily was out of the mirror, which was an extremely big tick. But I did not feel like celebrating. She was tiny and translucent and terribly sad. In my imagination, she came out all shiny and normal and stayed that way. My imagination was in shock from reality.

What had I done?

In all the commotion, Mum and Dad woke up and were like, 'What is going on?' just as the rest of my family walked in from their little park walk.

It was me who cried out, 'Nimmy has just died!' to help everyone come up to speed with the fact. There was a lot of crying and talking and phone calls to be made, cake to be eaten and tea to be drunk. The Rosy Room felt crowded and I began to feel squashed and small and tragic. I started to chant, *It will be alright Lily,* and Mum thought I was giving myself a weird pep talk but I wasn't, I was just trying to reassure OL whose face flashed between a picture of rusted roses and the list of quality chocolates, which included a tempting soft-centred selection. Yum. (I can't help it if I notice important details in the midst of a crisis.)

I looked into the chocolate tin and tried to smile because if I had just gotten out of a mirror after sixty-seven years then turned into a slippery little version of myself inside a chocolate tin that was chocolate-free and full of Beryl's old bits and pieces — I'd need some cheering. But truthfully … I was not sure how I was going to make it all right for OL.

I gazed intensely at Zinnia in an attempt to appear normal and not like I was clutching onto a tin full of supernatural goodness. I thought (hoped) Zinnia might burst into her usual loud tears and distract everyone so I could deal with the situation in my hands but surprisingly Zinnia did not cry. Instead she said something very nice in Spanish. She was looking at GG holding Nimmy and then she looked at Manuel and then she smiled at Fern. (Fern is learning Spanish to visit Zinnia soon.) Even though it sounded very beautiful, I thought she was saying, 'Would anyone care for a cup of tea?' because we do drink tea in a crisis. She kept on talking so I thought she added, 'It's a pity we have run out of milk,' but she didn't say that at all because the words made Manuel have a little cry too. He is a big softy — but I was sure he would not be blubbing over milk.

So we were all in and out of the Rosy Room for the next little bit. Then Sophie said it might be a good idea if we took Nimmy back to her bedroom so we did. GG and Mum hurried ahead as they wanted to remake the bed and open up the curtains etc etc. GG loved my roses and said, 'You are a very thoughtful young lady.' Dad and Mum tucked Nimmy up and GG sat down next to her. Then all my family stood or sat in GG and Nimmy's room to wait for the doctor and the matron and the non-sirened ambulance to come. It didn't take long … Treebark is pretty small.

The room was very quiet so we could hear the magpies singing and the dragonflies buzzing, which was really nice. But we could also hear HB's dogs going bonkers at the postman. Sigh!

I whispered to Zinnia, 'What did you say back in the Rosy Room?'

Zinnzy smiled and translated for us, 'Love is not a figment, it is alive and real and in this room.'

El amor no es una invención. Es un ser vivo y real, y está presente aquí en esta habitación.

Surprisingly Linden blubbed like the rest of us.

Mum squeezed Dad's hand and he smiled at her like he met her last week and not over twenty-five years ago, which was nice but nauseating too.

This veritable love-fest made me think of poor OL who was still in my tin. Or I thought she was! I looked down and she wasn't there. My brain went into total overdrive but I had the presence of mind not to scream out loud *WHERE IN THE BLAZES ARE YOU, LILY?*

I looked hard into the tin willing her to pop back into my sight. I stared so hard I felt hot tears blur the picture on the lid. The red and yellow roses became blobs of orange and the word *Cadbury* became *Farbslurry*. Not as appealing.

I kept my eyelids half shut and squinted down mournfully at the rug. The tassles at the end of the rug started to twitch and before I could think *the pesky mice are back* I caught sight of a foot wearing a sensible sandal and missing a toe.

OL had slid out of the tin and into the drapes. They were a faded chintz pattern and her image made the material shimmer like a cloudy flowerbed.

Breathtakingly beautiful but utterly woebegone. (Linden, family Scrabble loser three years running, argued *woebegone* was not a word. Seriously!)

It now appeared Other Lily could stretch or shrink to match the shape and size of her support vehicle.

I was wishing for my sensible Hermione to come back but I couldn't even muster Dobby the house elf.

I watched Other Lily stare at her dear one and attempt a brave but shaky smile just for me. But the wobble turned into a wiggle and the wiggle became a jiggle. The curtain started to bounce and twitch and Fern stood up to shut the window. But it was, of course, closed. Draughts and old people are mutually exclusive. Fern did her *that is a curious thing* frown but said nothing. Thank goodness! I watched as OL slid into the floorboards and out of sight.

The doctor came and he had heaps of questions for Sophie and GG. Mum and Dad stayed and helped GG sign some forms (he was a bit shaky) but the rest of us went into the kitchen and Zinnia put the kettle on (typical Griffin procedure). We wanted to give Nimmy some privacy for the last part of her journey.

At first there was a lot of confusion in the kitchen: Where are the special herbal tea bags? (Fern) Where is the decaf? (Zinnia) Why does GG insist on drinking goat milk? (Linden) I found the proper milk! (me) Please — I need coffee right now! (Zinnia) Who ate the last piece of chocolate ganache cake? (Pig Boy) And yes … it was me in a moment of panic … BLUSH. Everyone blustered around, trying to be upbeat about Nimmy having a long and pretty awesome life.

I overheard Zinnia saying she was going to bake some scones as the cake tin was empty and I got distracted for a minute or two. They are simply the best and their comfort factor is like … a thousand.

But then I couldn't find OL and I was really scared some more bad magic had happened to her and she had disappeared forever.

I went back into the Rosy Room but the mirror just looked like an ordinary old mirror. I carefully threw over the dust cloth for the last time.

My vibe kicked in and it grew stronger and stronger as I walked down the passage and entered the good room. Other Lily was there, twisted around the wooden hatstand like a gorgeous scarecrow so she could support herself to look out the window. She was watching the ambulance drive away. She didn't notice me. I stepped back into the hallway and the burbling noise of my family struck me — yes, loud and annoying, but well … I was glad my awesome family was in the next room.

Thinking about my own family made me think OL would never see or talk to hers again. All of us were her family as well but unless we all knew the truth, there would be more secrets … and she might be forgotten. I was glued to the spot. I could not leave OL but I could not join my family.

The kitchen door opened a crack. Linden came out into the passage and shut the door behind him which, I guess, was thoughtful of him. He stood next to me and watched Other Lily staring at the rose garden that was blooming brilliantly with bees buzzing all around. It was a veritable riot of pinkness but even vibe-free Linden got the vibe she was not enjoying it.

'She is flat like that boy … in that book … remember?'

'Book?' I said on the verge of a total breakdown.

'Yeah, it's a little kids' book, *Flat Stanley*, remember Mum would read it to us all the time.'

This is probably about the last time he touched a book. I was four and he was nearly EIGHT.

Just saying.

So we had a 'moment' which was nice but then he caught sight of OL's hand and saw the spot where a finger should reside. And then I could actually see his brain go CHA-CHING because next thing I knew, he shouted at me, 'I KNEW IT! I KNEW YOU WERE INVOLVED SOMEHOW,' and then I could see his brain deciding if he was going to go nuts or not. Meanwhile he could not help but blurt out, 'What happened to your finger?'

OL snapped to attention and shouted boldly back at Linden, 'Listen here, chum (said in a non-chummy tone), you leave Lily alone. Do you understand, Bacon Brat!' She lifted her hand from the hatstand to point her finger at him. At first she dipped and swayed to the ground like a kite without wind but then she straightened herself up, clenched her fist and shook it with ferocity.

'It's *Pig Boy*,' I whispered while trying not to laugh and then I blinked innocently and said, 'Involved with what, Linden? Please don't be so erroneous.'

The pudding head stopped in his tracks and

looked rather confused. He had seen a finger do a disco solo and a pretty girl pulled out of a mirror. He had witnessed very good magic, the best kind of magic … magic of epic Harry-Potter-book-seven proportions. He looked bamboozled and then thoughtful … and it really suited him.

Just then Dad poked his head out the kitchen door and said, 'What is going on here? He eyeballed Linden in an authoritive way like *eyes on you, Sonny Jim*.

But Linden smiled (gasp) at me and said, 'Touché, Lily, touché.' (This is a Griffin-ism for you are right, well said or, in this case, well done.)

'Touché to what?' quizzed Dad. He was obviously shocked that Linden was being nice to me.

Linden looked at me and opened his mouth to say something when an almighty crack came from the Rosy Room.

Everyone rushed out of the kitchen and GG thought the ceiling might have fallen down, like it did in the laundry last spring (*a plurry nuisance!*) but we were not greeted by a big plastery powdery mess at our feet.

It was the mirror.

It was vibrating and wobbling like crazy. The aerogrammes that I had left out to read later glided around the room like pretty blue fairywrens. Everyone watched and nobody spoke — very weird for my family.

I thought for one spooky moment that Mock Cream Beryl was going to pop in but that would have been ridiculous and, as it turned out, completely erroneous. The drawers beneath the mirror rumbled forward and then the middle one — the one I had popped OL's finger and toe into — flew out and landed at my feet.

The entire family and Sophie were now crowded into the room. I could see OL's face glowing out of the large silver door handle. She winked at me.

Linden hid behind one of the big wingback chairs. Zinnia wailed loudly that the whole day was getting much too much for her and Fern stepped forward and said, 'Speak to us, o visiting spiritual guide … teach us your ways.' And even though we had been full of family love two minutes ago, Mum said, 'SHUTUP FERN — don't frighten Lily … Lily sweetie, it's just the house falling off the stumps.'

Dad shook his head and lifted his glasses before he shouted, 'THERE ARE NO SUCH THINGS AS GHOSTS!'

But then the dust cloth lifted and twirled up to the ceiling rose and swayed and swished. And everyone's faces were saying that no amount of termites and old wood could make the sheet dance on the ceiling. I have to say that it was mesmerising, utterly spectacular and beyond frightening. I almost need a new word to describe just this moment. Then the dust cloth fell on Linden's head and he started screaming. (I would like to say 'like a stuck pig' but I am working on my relationship with him. Kind of!)

Dad pulled him up off the floor and that is when we heard the second crack. The mirror was splitting into pieces. It was like watching ice break open on a frozen pond (in the movies … sadly there is no snow in Treebark). The glass turned into crazy geometric patterns and then each piece of the pattern started to crumble again until finally the glass was like a sheet of crystals … and then even the crystals became powdery like sand.

'DON'T TOUCH IT!' I screamed, 'EDGAR THE POLTERGEIST CREATED A VORTEX THAT TRAPPED OTHER LILY FOR SIXTY-SEVEN YEARS BECAUSE HE WAS SWEET ON LUCY — I MEAN NIMMY!'

'CALM DOWN, LILY,' shouted Dad in a completely agitated way. (Shouting at someone to 'calm down' when they are stressed is plain dumb.)

The glittery powder started to slide down and I thought once the powder hit the floorboards, we would all be trapped inside grains of powdery mirror. 'LET'S GET OUT OF HERE,' I screamed, feeling beyond *highly suggestible* and steamrolling into *highly charged*. But as the twinkly powder touched the ground … it disappeared. It just evaporated until soon the whole mirror had vanished and we were left with a very nice frame.

Something sashayed down from the ceiling and floated to Dad's feet. He picked it up and cried, 'It's Mum's handwriting,' as he wiped his tears with the back of his cardigan sleeve. His hand wobbled and a book fell to the ground. Of course, I was the only one with the presence of mind to pick it up.

Sixteen

It was one of Beryl's old notepads. On the first page Beryl had set down 'ten terrific ways with tripe'. Nimmy had scratched it out and had written *Setting Lily Free.* Dad had no idea what it meant and tried his best to put a sensible spin on it while I flicked through Nimmy's writing. The rest of the notepad was all about her ideas for getting Other Lily out of the mirror. Her handwriting started off way messy and then it got all small and loopy and grown up — like on the aerogrammes. She had scribbled Edgar's curse over and over like she was trying to work out what special clue she was missing. She had written down all the possible phrases that might undo it.

Of course nothing had worked but she must have had the vibe that the time was right, right now. The gift of *VIBE* is a totally underrated powerful thing. It is mighty MIGHTY.

Nimmy must have kept her secret thoughts stuck behind the mirror. A place where Other Lily could not see and Beryl would not dare to look!

'I'm sure there is a reasonable explanation,' said Dad in a voice that did not sound rational but squeaky and weird.

GG pushed his glasses back up on his nose and said, 'PISH POSH, JOHN, we just witnessed something supernatural and it was a magnificent display of … of what I don't know, but it surely was not rational or logical.' GG gulped and I could see his tears were about to spill out from under his ultra-daggy spectacles. The thick glass made them look like a weir about to gush over. He attempted my favourite classic Colin smile but failed. 'When my dear Lucy …' he could not say the word *died* so he said, 'When my dear heart took leave of the Rosy

Room, I could have sworn … I could have sworn I saw her younger self … not quite herself … a different self.'

Then he looked at me with big watery eyes as the penny began to drop *clang clangity clang*. The telepatheticness between us was electrifying. His big wide eyes said, *MISSING KEY + THE CLEVER COVER OF A COMPENDIUM OF RECIPES + FREAKED-OUT FAVOURITE GRANDCHILD ENSCONSED IN VINTAGE PARADISE = THE MISSING SISTER LILY.*

'Lily? It was Lily. It is Lily. Lily Dunnings!' he whispered, 'Lily Pilly, is she here now?'

Everyone's faces said, 'Oh dear, GG has totally flipped out!!'

But I said, 'YES, YES SHE IS!'

Grandad's legs swayed and buckled and Fern ran towards him to keep him from keeling over. She sat him down in Ken's chair.

My Grandad is made of strong stuff.

'Before my Lucy went into the Home, she would talk incessantly to the mirror — any mirror — and

I presumed it was part of her … condition. I paid no heed but I now know she was talking to her own dear sister … all this time … all those years.' GG was very brave and continued on. 'To me the mirror always seemed … I don't know how to say this. I was jealous of dear Lucy's strange fascination with it. I found it quite unsettling … it was always covered up and Lucy dearest would squeal with rage if I so much as stepped a foot near it, particularly if she was in the process of throwing the sheet over it. I have to admit that sometimes I was slightly miffed by her maudlin preoccupation with things from her past. But now I understand. I just wish she had told me.' GG's voice cracked and fell silent until he blew his nose trumpet-style on his gentleman-sized old hankie and tried to smile.

Dad was shaking his head and trying to talk but no words came out of his mouth. His mother had passed on and he thought his father was booking into cuckoo lalaland all in the same day. Poor Dad.

'You know I always got a strange feeling as well, GG,' said Fern, 'like the mirror was trying to draw me to it … as irresistible as the needle on the curse-ed spinning wheel.'

Whatever — I said to myself. I watched OL move from the shiny silver door handle and into the glass window, making sure this time she did not ruffle the sheer voile lace.

Am I the only one in the family who has any powers of observation at all?

'And just then in your bedroom I felt the drapes were possessed by a dreamy melancholy.' Fern began to tear up to show how overwhelming her gift of vibe is.

Annoying MUCH? (Although melancholy is an excellent word.)

I scowled at her and Mum saw me and tilted her head at Fern then back to me. This is Mum's code for *You are affecting Lily's mental health. Please stop ASAP.*

Fern scowled but shut up. It is so like Fern to want to be all in on the dark-and-mysterious thing. It is my thing. Stick to cats!

'Thank you, dear Frondsy,' smiled GG at Fern. This is his pet name for her. Mine is better.

Dad recovered and crossed his arms. He looked

a bit like Linden when he gets into trouble. 'Now, Dad … you are overwrought,' he said in his *I am humouring you* voice.

I knew it was up to me to speak up for Lucy and Other Lily and Colin. As I took a deep breath in, a vision of a young Nimmy popped into my head and she said, 'Finger fun time, dear Lily.'

So I bent down, intending to pick up the finger and the pin box with the toe bit in it. But the pin box snapped open ON ITS OWN and the toe bit left the pretty pinhead pins nest and moved forward up into the air and before my Dad could say, 'Go to your rational place and think logically,' the finger started to wiggle and jiggle and then it flew up to join the toe.

I turned to OL and said, 'Are you doing this?'

She shook her head and said, 'Golly gosh NO!' Her eyes were as big as my Dad's. 'But I know who is!'

Everyone turned at the sound of her charming voice ringing out of the lace.

Their eyes became as wide as orbs because they could all see a lovely vintage teen girl in the window. The lacy voile shimmered and it really suited her …

quite atmospheric. The best thing was she was no longer downhearted — she was beaming with sheer joy and chuckling. She waved and curtsied politely at us all but her eyes were glued on the floating finger and toe.

We followed her gaze and the eight of us slipped into a highly mesmerised state as the finger and toe literally tangoed and twisted midair in front of Dad's nose and then … *whoosh* they flew and flittered and flounced all the way to the windowpane and the voile parted by MAGIC.

The body parts settled onto OL's missing finger hand and damaged toe foot. OL giggled loudly and I thought this was way inappropriate at the time, until she whispered, 'Thank you, dear Lucy.' She moved her hand in a way that made me think she was touching dear Lucy's pretty ghostly face. Nimmy had fixed everything and given her dear sensible son John a bit of a fright. It was if she was saying, 'Go to your magical creative place and think of endless possibilities … and piffle to logic every now and then.'

Other Lily held out her hand and stepped out

of the window all freshly refreshed. As she became clearer, someone of equal beauty began to materialise. Other Lily was holding a young Lucy's hand! AKA our dear Nimmy.

Lucy/Nimmy was totally gorgeous. She had very straight blonde hair (exactly the same as mine except for the blonde bit) and she was rocking an emerald-green frock with a snazzy crocheted trim (a Beryl original). On her feet was a pair of sandals of a strappy nature, not in the least bit sensible, and quite sassy. I could not be sure but I thought she had on the slightest smear of a coral-coloured lipstick.

The sisters shimmied over to me. 'Thank you, dear Lily, for reuniting us after all these years. We could not have done it without you, you perfect peach,' trilled Nimmy.

I was bursting with sheer joy and I have to say it is the best, *best* feeling in the world.

Other Lily's blue eyes watered up with tears of happiness and she whispered, 'Two sisters — together again.'

I think Nimmy/Lucy must have felt extra chatty

and excited because she could now think and say what she needed to think and say for the first time in years.

She glided over to Zinnia. 'Zinnzy darling, ENJOY!' and she touselled Manuel's curls.

Then it was Fern's turn. 'Frondsy, FOCUS!' She playfully tweaked her nose.

She appeared in front of Mum and said, 'Letty sweetheart, COURAGE!'

Then she hurried over to her only son, my dad. 'John, RELAX!' She rubbed his belly.

Then she marched over to Pig Boy. 'Linden dearest, BUCK UP, BUCKO!' She poked him in the chest. I could tell it was not a hard poke but Linden jumped back like a scaredy-cat and stood on my toe.

Just saying.

She looked at Sophie and said, 'Thank you for having faith in Lily and for your devotion to me.'

Then it was my turn. 'Lily Pilly, you are a sheer delight,' she squeezed my hand and whispered, 'Life … EMBRACE!'

Finally she shimmied over to GG. 'Colin, my

dreamboat — my love.' She kissed his cheek tenderly and I was right about the lipstick … GG's cheek is still glowing.

She returned to Other Lily's side and said, 'Well, dear heart, we have a bit of time up our spectral sleeves … where to now?'

And as quick as a flash Other Lily replied, 'Papa's rose garden, of course, I noticed the Queen Elizabeth grandiflora was exquisite — but it wasn't the same without you, dear.'

They flew and glided over our heads and out into the glorious day. We could hear them giggling above the rose petals. We followed them outside to catch sight of the two gliding higher and higher.

Lucy squealed with a hint of wicked glee, 'Oh Lily darling, let's pay a visit to Dawn and get her sorted once and for all. We must — simply must — help her darling dogs.'

'We might kill her with the fright!' gasped OL at first but then began to titter, 'or just hospitalise her for a short spell. To save the pooches I think that is an acceptable risk! Smelling salts at the ready!'

OL turned to wave at me for the last time. She blew me a kiss as she cried out, 'If you need us, call on us!'

'How?' I shouted.

'You'll know,' laughed Nimmy, 'you are a very special and very smart girl!'

Higher and higher they flew until I could not see them but could just make out Nimmy's voice. 'How about Paris after that?'

'Jadorable,' was Other Lily's faint but dreamy reply.

The absolute best thing is that my entire family and Sophie the super-nice nurse (who is now our dear friend) SAW the entire thing. Not a product of Lily Land, father dearest!

After the magic slash supernatural fun finished, we all ended up back in the kitchen and Zinnia put the kettle on and started to make the scones.

Mum, Fern and I settled down in the Rosy Room

to go through all the tins and boxes. We were looking at old photos and cards and reading about all the wonderful memories. Mum found the copy of *Alice in Wonderland* hidden behind the wardrobe, double-wrapped in grease-proof paper with a kitchen string triple knot — sly Nimmy! When Fern found a picture of Fabian the cat she shouted, 'OMG — I forgot to feed the cats.'

The three cats were going off their white-and-red furry faces.

Fern opened the laundry door and screamed before bolting outside and running down the road shouting at the sky, 'Thank you, Nimmy and Aunty Lil.'

('The utter nerve … her name is LILY not LIL.)

I figured out why she was happy slash hysterical as the three cats strode into the Rosy Room and began to smooch and cuddle around my feet. They had completely returned to a normal sparkly white.

Amazeballs!

Everyone had so many questions and they were all talking at once so I went and got this diary and read it aloud for them while they were all sitting around the table. I left some bits out about me being scared at first, but I did not leave out anything that had to do with Linden!

He put his head down and chewed on his scone in a state of total embarrassment. Then he whispered, 'Sorry, Lily … for everything.' Mum was like, over the moon that he had said sorry, and even though I have kindly forgiven him, I can't help it if I have a really good memory. It is actually one of my strengths … along with my vibe gift.

GG wanted to read this journal for himself and has very nicely let me keep any letters and photos and material and newspaper clippings I want. I am going to glue them into the back of the notebook. GG said this is called an appendix. I do not like this word as it makes me think of a person's appendix. I prefer the word scrapbook. Mum is mad for scrapbooking, so she said she would help me arrange it all so it looks great and I can even use her hot-glue gun and double-sided tape — quite a breakthrough. (Letty/hot-glue gun = Beryl/creepy scissors, I do not understand how adults become so attached to boring everyday things!)

This reminds me, Dad was cool about the laptop damage. He said 'these things happen' (and did not add 'mostly to you, Lily' like he normally does). Apparently it is still under warranty. PHEW!

Fern is not smart like me but she is kind (I suppose) and is going to stay on to look after GG who has apparently been knocked for six (Dad-ism for *totally shocked*!).

Linden is still being nice but I won't waste my last pacer lead on him as I am nearly out of lead and want to finish this journal. We walked down to the shops together for milk, butter and choc bits so GG could make the ganache cake. He did not run away with all the money like he did last time so I dare to hope.

This morning Zinnia started screaming in Spanish from the bathroom. As it turns out, Zinnia's screams were happy screams because she and Manuel are having a baby! I thought I would be grossed out but I am not. I'm going to be an aunty. Amazeballs! Everyone is over the moon and it's the second best thing to happen this week.

I think my life is about to change.

I overheard Dad say that realistically he is not getting any younger as he is closer to sixty than fifty which is way old — and maybe they should think about retiring to Treebark. Mum said something about a *tree change* and a *complete re-evaluation of life values*. She said she finally felt ready to find her birth mother.

Zinnia told them that she and Manuel want their baby to grow up in Treebark. Then Fern piped up and said she didn't want to do Arts anymore, she wanted to be a wildlife rescue officer and Treebark is the perfect place for her as it is her ancestral village. *Spew! Sigh! Spew again!*

We were still in a joyous commotion when the doorbell rang.

I ran to answer it because I hoped it was the new

and improved Dawn. But it wasn't. It was Isabella, the girl from next door, with her dad. She was carrying a massive big bunch of old-fashioned flowers and they both wanted to tell GG they were there for him. Bless!

Isabella was wearing a Harry Potter t-shirt that had the words *Wizard in Training* printed on it. I have seen the shirt before on the internet and always wanted one. My intuition shouted YOU ARE AWESOME!

I asked her, 'You like Harry Potter?'

She smiled shyly and answered, 'It is my life.'

GG smiled at both of us and then invited the pair of them in for a cup of tea but Isabella's dad said that it was Issy's eleventh birthday and they were travelling to Perth to visit a special bookshop which is totes my favourite too!

I really hope we move here.

Mum and Dad told Zinnia and Fern 'not to mention it to Lily' as they do not want 'to overstimulate her' at this point in time. They have never seen me so chatty and happy and I guess it's freaking them out a bit. But my vibe is super strong that we will all be moving here very very soon! Hooray!

I brought my pacer and this journal into the Rosy Room as I thought I should write the last words in here. I was sitting on the rug and looking around wistfully when I got a very strong vibe to open up a certain shoebox, I was seriously overcome. So I opened up the box and all I saw were piles of baby photos of us all. There was a cute one of a bald Zinnzy cutting her first tooth, Fern has medieval-style braces on in one photo and Linden is wearing an elf suit that is clearly chafing in another. I am jadorable blowing out candles on my sixth birthday cake, with Nimmy's scaly old hand on top of mine, holding onto the knife. I had to stop for a while because of the lump in my throat.

I persevered with my divination and dug around to the bottom when my fingers touched a small wooden box. It is tiny and carved with the most glorious patterns. It has a beautiful smell — like lilies. I feel it is not part of the Rosy Room but it has a story of its own. I can't work out a way to open it up. It looks like a smooth square but when I rattle the box I can hear something move inside.

Diamonds?

I don't think so.

Intrigue and mystery?

I know so. I can feel in it my very core.

Lily Griffin

#mightyvibe #verygoodmagic #wordnerd

Acknowledgements

I would like to thank my aunt, Betty Prendergast, for the countless hours of proofreading and for the forty-five years of love.

Thank you to Cate Sutherland for seeing and understanding Lily's totes special internal landscape.

To my editor Naama, you have gently guided me through Lily's land and helped me to make it more accessible and wonderful! Thank you.

Thanks to my mum, dad and my own sister Linda and the Richos for all your love and support.

Thank you to Rebecca Newman for saying 'what Cate said' and pointing me in the right direction.

Catherine Parish (AKA Kate Martyn), Jean Prendergast and Anna Nankivell — thanks for your never-ending kind words.

To Wendy Wright — for getting it and loving it.

To Elle Lambert and her dad, an inspirational duo.

And for June Roberts — there is beauty in the littlest things.

To Phil, Luke, Angela, Charlotte and Daniel — you all inspire me, each with your own strengths and gifts.

About the Author

Paula Hayes is an introverted mother of four who tends to collect small animals. Writing has always been her passion but it had been sadly tempered by her gift for procrastination. She does not like sudoku, board games or heights. She is recovering from a deep-seated fear of figs.